PUFFIN BOOKS

THE DOWNHILL CROCODILE WHIZZ
AND OTHER STORIES

Here is a marvellous collection of Margaret Mahy's lively, zany and inventive stories featuring all sorts of unusual characters. There's Weedy Deedee, the orphan with the biggest feet in the world; Ethelred, the boy who is ready for absolutely anything; Minnie, the girl with the magical green ear who can understand the language of plants; and of course, the unstoppable roller-skating crocodile.

'Another dazzling confection of stories from a master storyteller . . . this book will be relished by children – and their parents' – *Books for Your Children*

Margaret Mahy is a New Zealander who has been writing stories from the age of seven. She has been awarded the Carnegie Medal twice and the Esther Glen Award three times. She has two grown-up daughters, several cats, a large garden and thousands of books. She lives near Christchurch, South Island. Margaret Mahy's books for Puffin include *Raging Robots and Unruly Uncles* and *A Lion in the Meadow* (Picture Puffin).

Margaret Mahy

THE DOWNHILL CROCODILE WHIZZ AND OTHER STORIES

———— ☼ ————

Illustrated by Jon Riley

PUFFIN BOOKS

PUFFIN BOOKS

Published by the Penguin Group
27 Wrights Lane, London w8 5tz, England
Viking Penguin Inc., 40 West 23rd Street, New York, New York 10010, USA
Penguin Books Australia Ltd, Ringwood, Victoria, Australia
Penguin Books Canada Ltd, 2801 John Street, Markham, Ontario, Canada L3R 1B4
Penguin Books (NZ) Ltd, 182–190 Wairau Road, Auckland 10, New Zealand

Penguin Books Ltd, Registered Offices: Harmondsworth, Middlesex, England

First published by J. M. Dent & Sons Ltd, 1986
Published in Puffin Books 1987
Reprinted 1988

Text copyright © Margaret Mahy, 1986
Illustrations copyright © Jon Riley, 1987
All rights reserved

Made and printed in Great Britain by
Richard Clay Ltd, Bungay, Suffolk
Filmset in Monophoto Photina

CONTENTS

THE DOWNHILL
CROCODILE WHIZZ

— ☼ —

One day a small crocodile received an unexpected present for his last birthday but one. It was from his grandmother who was away somewhere leading a very spritely life of her own. The crocodile felt the parcel all over, trying to guess what might be inside it.

'She's sent me shoes,' said the crocodile in a slightly disappointed voice. But it was not shoes. It was a pair of roller-skates and a letter.

'Dear Grandson,' said the letter, 'I am sending you my old roller-skates because I am giving up skating and taking up hang-gliding instead. Look after these skates very well, won't you, because they are good ones. On these very skates I won the Ladies All-in Skating Championship of Orinocco. I am afraid you will never be the skater that I am, but you might as well have a go. Happy birthday for your last birthday but one. Your devoted Grandmother.' Then at the very end of the letter it said, 'P T O' which stands for *Please Turn Over*, but the crocodile did not notice this.

'What does she mean, I'll never be the skater that she is?' he cried. 'Great Granglenuckers! As if I couldn't skate better than an old woman crocodile of ninety-two.' He dropped the letter and began studying the skates. 'I see. You strap them on to your paws. Simple!'

He put the skates on straight away and stood up very confidently. Then he had to stand up all over again. Next he shot across the room and found he was lying on his back with the skates in the air.

'Funny!' mused the crocodile. 'I wonder how that happened?'

At last he managed to stand up and stay standing up, balancing cleverly with his tail.

'There you are . . . Easy!' said the crocodile in rather a bruised voice. 'Now I'm going to have a go outside. Somehow I have a feeling I'm going to be a singularly splendid skater.'

As it happened, the crocodile lived at the very top of a very steep hill. There was absolutely nowhere to go in any direction but DOWN. So the crocodile pointed his feet, in his grandmother's skates, in the direction of down . . . simply to have a go. WHIZZZZ! Off he went, balancing majestically with his fine tail.

It's easy! thought the crocodile. I don't see what all the fuss is about. The skates do it all for you. He went faster and faster. WHIZZZ!

A little girl called Katy was sitting in front of her gate on a tricycle. Her mother had told her never to go out of the gate because of the steepness of the hill outside, but when she saw the crocodile going past, she couldn't resist joining in too.

WHIZZZ! went the crocodile. WHIZZZZZ! went Katy.

'Isn't it fun?' yelled Katy. 'I'll stop when you do.'

'I don't think I'll be stopping for a while,' the crocodile cried in an anxious voice. 'I've just found out that these skates aren't the sort of skates that have brakes.' They went faster and faster. Two dogs were pulling a rubbish bag to pieces, but they stopped to watch Katy and the crocodile go by.

'*They're* having fun,' barked Black Dog.

'Let's go along too, shall we?' said Spotted Dog. 'This rubbish bag is a very disappointing one.' So the two dogs joined in too, wagging their tails and waving their tongues as they ran. WHIZZZZ! WHIZZZZZ! WAG! WAG!

When they were further down the hill they came across rich old Mr Whisker tucked into his wheelchair, being wheeled across the footpath to his car by his dashing nurse who was called Nurse Frolic. A chauffeur was holding the car door open and bowing, but unfortunately as Katy and the crocodile whizzed by they brushed against the wheelchair which spun round three times and then joined in the downhill whizz-and-wag procession.

'Isn't it fun?' Katy called to Mr Whisker.

'Hooray! Here we go!' he shouted most enthusiastically, glad to get away from Nurse Frolic and the chauffeur who were both very bossy and always said they were only bossy for his own good.

3

'I'm going to stop when the crocodile stops,' shouted Katy.

'So am I!' agreed Mr Whisker. 'These crocodiles know a thing or two.'

'I won't be stopping immediately,' mumbled the crocodile desperately, balancing with his tail for all he was worth and making circles in the air with his short front legs.

'Isn't he clever?' yapped Black Dog.

'Yes,' panted Spotted Dog. 'He keeps pretending he's going to fall over and then he never quite does.'

They went faster and faster, while behind them, shouting and yelling, ran Katy's mother, Nurse Frolic and the chauffeur.

About halfway down the hill they came upon Mrs Harris leaning out of the window and telling her husband which apples to buy at the greengrocer's. She was holding their baby – a fine boy named Sampson.

'Not those green ones,' she was saying, 'and not the very red ones . . .'

But just then she heard a whizzing sound and saw the crocodile, Katy, Mr Whisker, Black Dog, Spotted Dog – thirteen wheels and eight paws – all speeding towards her. She got a terrible fright.

'Awwwk!' she screamed and – dropped the baby.

Luckily, as the crocodile shot under her window, waving his short little arms, he just happened to catch little Sampson and carried him off at great speed.

WHIZZZ! went the crocodile and Sampson. WHIZZZ! went Katy. WHIZZZZ! went Mr Whisker. WAG-WAG went Black Dog. WAG-WAG went Spotted Dog. 'Stop! Stop! STOP! STOP!' shouted Katy's mother, Nurse Frolic, the chauffeur and the Harrises who joined in, running faster than the others because they were so upset to see their baby carried off by a crocodile.

A brass band in a bus turned into the road on its way down to the park at the bottom of the hill where it was going to play that very afternoon.

'Look! A downhill crocodile whizz!' exclaimed the bandmaster, leaping from his seat and reaching for his baton. 'Let's give them a bit of an oom pah pah! Ready boys? *Prestissimo accelerando!*'

The band began to play 'Land of Hope and Glory' with all the *prestissimo* and *accelerando* that a heart could desire. They opened the windows for the trombones and the driver speeded up a little bit so that they could keep up with the crocodile who, by now, was going downhill very fast indeed.

Up in a tall building in the heart of the city, a military man called General Confusion was pacing up and down impatiently. Every now and then he looked out of the window, swore, and went back to his impatience and his pacing. It was years and years and years since there had been a war and he was very cross about it. He had had a grand uniform and a whole army for years and years and years, and absolutely nothing had happened. Then, as he looked out of the window he thought he saw something ominous whizzing down the hill as if it were about to launch an attack on the park gates.

'Enemies! At last!' shouted General Confusion. 'We are being invaded.' Then he took his brass bugle, leaned out of the window, and blew a gallant blast on it. *Taranta ra! Taranta ra!* Out rushed the majors and the captains, and the sergeant majors, and the ordinary soldiers – all armed with bazookas and blunderbusses and ready for battle and bloodshed.

'FORWARD!' shouted the General. 'Defend the bottom of the hill! Protect the gates of our lovely civic park!' As one soldier the army charged towards the bottom of the hill.

'There goes the army!' everyone said. 'There's going to be a battle.' There was great excitement, and everyone held up their babies and aged parents so that they could get a good view too. WHIZZZZ! went the crocodile. He was going so fast that he was absolutely numb with terror. Katy followed behind him, and everyone else just after her.

'Aren't you ever going to stop?' Katy shouted to the crocodile.

'Er . . .' said the crocodile.

'Look at him!' yelled Mr Whisker, waving his hearing-aid with admiration. 'He's skating on one foot . . . now he's skating on the other. What a croc, what a croc, what a crackerjack croc!'

'They're waiting for us,' cried Katy. 'We've become famous since we started off at the top of the hill.'

'Do you think we'd better stop?' asked Mr Whisker. 'We're going very fast. We don't want to run into anyone, and cause an accident.'

But the crocodile couldn't stop. WHIZZZZ! went his

grandmother's All-in-Champion-of-Orinocco skates. He swayed this way. He swayed that way. He balanced with his tail, and he tried to think what to do next. But there was only one thing he *could* do! Holding little Sampson high in the air to save him from any bumps and bruises, he shouted, 'Follow me!' and they did follow him, all of them.

WHIZZZZ! He whizzed right through the ranks of soldiers. The bazookas went one way and the blunderbusses went another. Luckily the park gates were open and the crocodile went right through the gates at about a hundred kilometres an hour, and then three times around the park, holding little Sampson Harris, who gurgled with delight and patted the crocodile's long, leathery snout. They were followed by Katy, Mr Whisker, Black Dog, Spotted Dog, Mr and Mrs Harris, Nurse Frolic, the chauffeur, Katy's mother, and a brass band in a bus playing like men inspired. People cheered, and so did their babies and their aged parents. It was the most interesting and inspiring incident to have taken place in that town for some time.

At last the crocodile was able to stop. He was quite out of breath what with trying to balance and looking after little Sampson Harris as well. But before he had time to settle down a bit, General Confusion was surrounding him with bruised soldiers and dented bazookas.

'Arrest that wicked crocodile!' he roared, pointing at the crocodile with his sword.

'No, don't!' cried another voice. 'Don't you dare lay a finger on that noble creature. That dear reptile has saved the life of our little Sampson.'

'What?' cried General Confusion, suddenly noticing the baby. 'He's saved the life of our little Sampson? What a spirited saurian! What a croc, what a croc, what a crackerjack croc!'

For Mrs Harris, before she had married Mr Harris, had been the beautiful Miss Confusion, the General's own

8

daughter, and so Sampson was the General's own grandson.

So the unexpected downhill crocodile whizz became an unexpected park party. Everyone had a lovely time, including the babies and the aged parents. The band played fit to bust, and the General pinned one of his medals on to the crocodile's waistcoat. Mr Whisker (who was *very rich*) said he would pay to have a bronze statue put up in the park, showing the crocodile balancing on one skate and catching baby Sampson in his short little arms.

Then Mr and Mrs Harris took Sampson home and General Confusion took the army home, Katy's mother took Katy home, Nurse Frolic and the chauffeur took Mr Whisker home, and the band took their bassoons and trombones home. And everyone else took their babies and aged parents and went home too.

But there was nobody to take the crocodile home. After slapping him on the back and waving goodbye, everybody left the crocodile standing in his grandmother's skates in the golden evening light.

That's all right! he thought. I'll skate home. It won't take long.

But he *couldn't* skate home. It was uphill all the way.

He had to walk uphill on his short little legs. Black Dog and Spotted Dog went with him most of the way, but then they saw a very promising rubbish bag and forgot about the crocodile who was all plodding and slow now. He wasn't nearly as much fun going uphill as he had been coming down.

At last the crocodile staggered in through his own front door at the very top of the hill dead beat, dog tired and done for. He collapsed into a chair and sat still for a long time, just breathing and blinking, breathing and blinking. Then he noticed his grandmother's birthday letter still on the table, and he saw that at the very end of the birthday letter she had written P T O which (as you know) means *Please Turn Over*. So the crocodile picked it up and P T O-ed.

'Dear Grandson,' his grandmother had written on the other side of the page. 'Whatever you do, WATCH OUT FOR HILLS! Your loving Grandmother.'

THE GIRL WITH THE GREEN EAR

The great conductor, Garfield Fortune, should have been a happy man. He had a good ear for music, as you could easily see, for his ears were shaped rather like violins. He could play not only the violin and the trombone, but knock out a good tune on the mouth organ as well. Every night he put on a black coat and conducted the city orchestra until he was completely worn out and had to be sent home in a taxi. Other musicians gave him envious looks when they saw him in the street.

'What a successful man!' they sighed. 'Not only has he got musical ears, but he has a fine house so full of flourishing pot plants it looks like a tropical rain forest. And, besides all that, he has a beautiful daughter called Minnie.'

They did not know that Minnie was causing her father a lot of trouble. She was breaking his heart.

'You are breaking my heart,' he said bitterly.

Garfield Fortune wanted Minnie to learn to play the french horn, but she tossed her golden curls and refused to do so. Some girls are like that. Whenever their fathers want them to do something (and all for their own good), they decide to do the opposite. It was natural that a man like Garfield Fortune should want his daughter to be musical, and the town orchestra badly needed someone to play the french horn. Their usual horn player V. G. Sevenby

had entirely disappeared and no one knew where to find him.

'The orchestra is not the same without a french horn!' cried Garfield Fortune. 'Minnie, you could pick up the french horn in next to no time if only you would let me give you a lesson or two.'

'But I don't want to be musical!' cried Minnie. 'I want to lead a strange, adventurous life. I want to do something different from you.'

'I command you to take french horn lessons,' shouted her angry father.

'No!' said Minnie boldly.

'You leave me no choice!' said Garfield Fortune coldly. 'I shall have to disown you.'

'The pot plants will go yellow without me,' Minnie declared.

'Go!' thundered her enraged father, 'and never darken my doors again.'

'Don't forget to water the pot plants,' begged Minnie. She went to her room and packed her toothbrush and her Post Office savings book. Then she set off into the big city. Garfield Fortune had not been expecting such bravery in a girl with golden curls and forget-me-not blue eyes. However, he was too proud to change his mind.

Minnie walked up and down the big city until she came to a rather rough street called Cabbage Row. As she wandered along it, a notice in a window caught her eye.

Isn't it lucky that I don't play the french horn! Minnie thought triumphantly. This is the very place for me. She knocked loudly at the door. When the landlord came Minnie could see at once, by his sad eyes, that he was a man with a secret sorrow. However, she did not try to find out what it was. She simply asked if he would let his bed-sitting room to her, even though she was not a retired gent.

'But are you sure you are not musical?' he asked, looking at her suspiciously in the evening light. 'You look as if you might be.'

'Certainly not!' said Minnie proudly.

'Then the room is yours,' he said. As he showed her to her room, Minnie couldn't help noticing that he had rather nice ears. They reminded her of something, but she couldn't think what it was.

Now she was starting a new life, Minnie thought she ought to look different in some way. I know, she decided at last, I must get my hair dyed green. My father will never recognize me with green hair.

Next to *The Harp and Banjo Hire Service* in the main street was a hairdressing salon – *Mr Plato's Hairstyles* – where Minnie asked about having her hair dyed green.

'What a good idea!' said the hairdresser, Mr Plato himself. 'I have a new dye I am longing to try, but my clients are foolishly nervous and shy.' Nevertheless, Mr Plato was very

13

careless for a man in charge of a powerful new dye. He kept talking to another hairdresser about what he was going to do during the weekend, and did not notice the green dye running down into Minnie's left ear. At the end of an hour Minnie's hair was a beautiful, bright green, and so was her ear, inside and outside. There was nothing that could be done about it, but luckily Minnie did not mind. Her father would never recognize her with a green ear as well as green hair. It was a perfect disguise.

Yet, no sooner was she outside in the street, than Minnie suddenly found she could hear all sorts of voices with her green ear, voices she could not hear with the ordinary pink one. She could hear the grass singing to itself, and the trees in the park murmuring in deep, sleepy voices. She could hear dandelions roaring, and weeds pushing up out of cracks in the city pavements, and she could hear the slow voice of the sea saying, 'Old! Old! Old!' as it fell on the beach on the edge of town. Everything that was green Minnie could hear with her green ear.

Close at hand a little voice was crying, 'Help! Help! Help!' very sadly, and another fierce voice was saying, 'Eat! Eat! Eat!'

'This needs looking into!' said Minnie, for she was a very brave girl.

Her green ear led her straight to a shop that specialized in pot plants. Most of the pot plants were looking well, and growing well. Some were like fountains, and some were like lace, and some were like green beads strung on threads of gold.

As she came in through the door one particular plant tried to grab her.

'You've got to watch that one!' said the plant shopman with a merry laugh. 'It is a rare, carnivorous plant, fresh from the jungle.'

'Do you mean it eats meat?' asked Minnie sternly.

14

'Only when it can get any,' said the plant shopman, 'but I have it firmly tied up. It had sausages for breakfast. I'm very kind to it.'

But Minnie was not interested in the wicked, carnivorous plant. She looked behind some tree ferns, and found a poor little pot plant looking very sorry for itself.

'What is the meaning of this?' asked Minnie pointing at it. 'You should look after your pot plants better than this.'

'Oh, that one just won't pull itself together,' whined the plant shopman. 'It won't try.'

'It needs kindness and encouragement,' Minnie told him.

'Oh well, if you think you can do better than me, buy it and see for yourself,' answered the heartless fellow with a mocking laugh.

'I will!' Minnie said, and she paid for the plant at once and carried it home with her. There, she put it on the windowsill, where it would have a good view of Cabbage Row.

The pot plant was grateful for its new home and the interesting view, but it had had a hard time at the plant shop, for the man had often forgotten to water it and the carnivorous plant had kept on whispering, 'Eat! Eat! Eat!' It promised Minnie that it would do its best to grow, but, though it tried hard, it dreamed of caterpillars and dryness and woke up terrified.

Minnie watered it and spoke to it kindly. 'When I was little and had bad dreams,' she said, 'my father would play to me on his violin. You need soothing watery music of some kind.'

As she said this she suddenly remembered the shop next to Mr Plato's – the one called *The Harp and Banjo Hire Service*.

'Don't worry!' she said to the plant. 'I have a plan. You'll be green and flourishing in next to no time.'

The very next day Minnie came home from town with a large, strangely shaped parcel. The landlord helped her carry it into her room.

'Are you sure you are not musical?' he asked, looking suspiciously at the parcel.

'Certainly not!' exclaimed Minnie. 'This is a sort of medicine for an ailing pot plant.'

Still, she waited until he had left the room before she opened it. Minnie had hired a large, golden harp carved all over with ivy and singing angels. She had also borrowed a book entitled *Beautiful Harp Playing in Three Easy* Lessons from the public library. Minnie turned to page one.

'This looks quite easy,' she said to the pot plant. 'Harp music is like beautiful silver rain. It's like waterfalls on the moon.'

'There is no water on the moon,' said the plant. (Plants know things like that by instinct. They don't need telescopes or astronomy books.)

'Well if there *were* waterfalls on the moon they would

16

sound like harp music,' Minnie said. She began to play at once, making a few mistakes but not very many considering she had never laid hand on a harp in her life before. She got on to page two in double quick time.

There was a knock at the door. It was the landlord.

'I'm sorry!' he said. 'You know the rules. No music.'

'Don't jump to conclusions,' said Minnie. 'This isn't real music. This is a pot-plant cure. This poor little pot plant has been having nightmares, and I am trying to help it.' The landlord apologized for his mistake. He really did have rather nice ears. Minnie realized they reminded her of french horns. They had the same neat, curly look.

'Go on curing the pot plant,' he said. 'I will bring you a soothing herbal tea and a plain biscuit.'

Minnie went on to page three. How beautiful she looked, her green curls contrasting vividly with the golden harp, her green ear standing out against the rest of her pearly skin. She ran her graceful fingers over the strings and wonderful sounds fell through the air like silver needles. As it listened, the pot plant relaxed, and actually put out a new leaf.

The landlord brought her supper, and sat listening to the lovely music, sipping his cup of herb tea very quietly so as not to disturb her.

'That's enough for tonight,' Minnie said. 'Lesson two tomorrow.'

The next day Minnie got up early, and put her head (with its green ear) out of the window of the bed-sitting room in Number Seven B. All over the city she could hear the voices of ailing pot plants grumbling to themselves.

'I have mapped out a career for myself,' Minnie told her own pot plant, and put a poster in her window. She also put a large advertisement in the paper. The poster and the advertisement said the same thing. This is what they said.

If your pot plant's had a fright
I'm the one to put it right!
If your pot plant's getting worse
I will be a loving nurse.
Rush sick pot plants round to me –
To Cabbage Row at Seven B.

'I wish I had a gift for poetry,' said the landlord wistfully.

'Caring for others brings out the best in us,' said Minnie modestly, looking admiringly at the landlord's neat, curling ears. She couldn't help wondering about them – they looked so musical.

By lunchtime a small queue had formed. Anxious pot-plant owners had rushed their ailing pot plants round for kindly advice. With her green ear Minnie was able to hear what the plants had to say, and was able to tell people exactly what the plants needed.

'Too much sun,' she said, or, 'Not enough sun!' or, 'This plant needs a steamy atmosphere. Put it in the bathroom, and take a hot bath three times a day.'

Severe cases were left overnight, and Minnie played the harp to them. She got through lesson two and then lesson three. Sometimes the plants joined in, in little green voices that only Minnie could hear.

One evening, about a week after she had arrived, the landlord came into her room holding a yellow book.

'Look,' he said in a casual voice. 'Look what I found upstairs when I was cleaning out the attic.'

The book was called, to Minnie's astonishment, *A Thousand Duets for Harp and French Horn*.

'Isn't that strange?' gasped Minnie. 'If only you had a french horn you could learn to play it and we could make lovely music together.'

'Just by a strange coincidence I find I do have a french horn in the attic,' said the landlord. 'I think I could easily learn to knock out a tune on it.'

'You aren't musical yourself, by any chance, are you?' asked Minnie sternly, for she thought she had had enough of musical people when living with her father.

'No! No!' cried the landlord. 'Perish the thought!'

'Very well, Virgil,' said Minnie (for such was the landlord's name), 'we will try these duets, but for medicinal reasons only. I am sure they will suit my pot plants down to the ground.'

That very evening, wonderful french horn and harp duets were heard in Cabbage Row, and a crowd collected outside Seven B, listening with rapture. Minnie's bed-sitting room was soon full of pot plants growing so tall and green that it was rather like being in a tropical rain forest.

Meanwhile, over on the other side of the city, Garfield Fortune was a dejected man. Firstly, he was missing Minnie, for now there was no one to argue with, and, secondly, the town orchestra was not doing at all well. People came to listen, but sometimes they would grow impatient and shout, 'Where's your french horn, eh?' and, 'What about a harp, then?' and other critical comments. These were sensitive music lovers who did not wish to hear Mozart's Horn Concerto played on a trombone.

Not only this, all the pot plants in Garfield's house had gone yellow. There was no fun in supping his evening sherry among a lot of yellowing vegetation. He picked up the evening paper, hoping that the usual bad news would make him feel better about his own miseries, and there before him was a big advertisement.

Rush sick pot plants round to me –
To Cabbage Row at Seven B.

Perhaps I could get this pot plant expert to make a house call, he thought. Cabbage Row is a very rough part of town. There are no musical people in Cabbage Row, and they all have cauliflower ears. Unfortunately, though, there was no phone number.

Meanwhile, Minnie was getting many commissions. She now had the job of looking after pot plants in the library, the bank, the town hall, and many leading restaurants. Not only this, she was asked to lecture on pot-plant restoration at the university. In spite of her fame, the times she enjoyed most were when she and Virgil played their duets to frail pot plants in the evening at Seven B Cabbage Row. They were up to duet number fifty-seven.

However, one evening their duet was interrupted. A police van passed down the street, with a tall policeman leaning out of the window and shouting through a megaphone, 'Attention! Attention! A fierce carnivorous pot plant has broken its chains and smashed down the door of the *Pot Luck Pot Plant Shop*. It was last seen making for Cabbage Row. All residents are advised to hide under their beds. Do not panic! If you hear screams, simply put your fingers in your ears and count to five thousand. This pot plant is savage – repeat *savage* – and should not be approached.'

'I certainly won't panic,' said Minnie, smiling at the mere

thought. 'Music hath powers to soothe the savage breast, and if that carnivorous pot plant should burst in here, we will give it a quick burst of duet number forty-two.'

'How brave you are!' exclaimed Virgil, staring at her adoringly, and looking very musical in spite of himself. 'A while ago life seemed empty of meaning. I had nothing to look forward to, except getting a bit of rent every so often, but now . . .'

'Oh!' cried the pot plant on the windowsill (Minnie's first pot plant, now fine and vigorous with many leaves), 'a stranger in a cloak is coming down Cabbage Row.'

'Does he look like a carnivorous pot plant disguised?' asked Minnie.

'No – he looks more like a sculptor or an artist or a famous conductor,' said the perceptive plant.

But at that very moment Minnie, with her green ear, heard a well-remembered voice saying, 'Eat! Eat! Eat!'

'Warn him!' she shouted. 'The carnivorous pot plant is lurking in the shadows. Virgil! Play "The Retreat" on your horn.'

Too late! There came a scream from the street below. The carnivorous pot plant, grown to monstrous dimensions on a diet of sausages, leaped out of hiding and wrapped its tendrils around the distinguished stranger. Bracing itself by curling its thick roots around a telegraph pole, the plant prepared to devour him.

But Minnie flung the window wide.

'Virgil – duet forty-two!' she cried, and a moment later a wonderful melody flooded out into the street. Up and down Cabbage Row, people who had been preparing to follow the instructions of the police van, and were about to fill their ears with cotton wool and climb under their beds, came out and began to listen instead. The horn was like a wonderful golden vine twining through the air, while the harp was like silver cobwebs, catching drops of a delicate rain and

holding them like pearls. Fortunately the carnivorous plant
was distracted. It appeared to stop and listen intently. Virgil
and Minnie played like people inspired. The music flooded
the street with feelings full of forgiveness, and hope for better
things to come. Even the victim, desperate though he was,
was deeply affected. His arms twitched, just as if he were
trying to conduct, despite the deadly embrace of a carnivorous pot plant. The music changed. It grew more powerful and reproachful, filled with grief for the wickedness of
the world. People wept, and the pot plant was deeply affected
too. It opened great, scarlet flowers, and tears of honey
dripped from them, showing plainly that the plant was
stricken with remorse. Slowly its tendrils relaxed.

'How wicked I have been,' Minnie heard it say, 'going
around saying, "Eat! Eat! Eat!" instead of giving my mind to
nobler things.' Though only Minnie could hear it, anyone in
Cabbage Row could see that it was sorry for what it had
done. It not only released its victim, but brushed him down
and gave his hat back to him.

'I forgive you,' the victim said, 'but I must find the players
of that heavenly music. I must thank my rescuers. I came
here to consult a pot-plant expert, for my pot plants are suffering from yellowness, but I have found truly musical people
in Cabbage Row.' Closely followed by the erstwhile carnivorous pot plant, he ran up the steps and burst through the door
of Seven B. Then he stood like one pierced by sudden arrows.

'My daughter Miniver,' he cried (for that was Minnie's
full name), 'and V. G. Sevenby, my missing french horn-
player! What are you doing in this tropical rain forest?'

'I live here,' said Virgil. 'My house is Seven B and so am I.
I have recovered my powers of french horn-playing, thanks
to the inspiration of your lovely daughter, whom I now ask
to marry me.'

'Oh, Minnie, Minnie!' wailed her father. 'How you have
suffered! I see your hair has gone green with suffering. Never

23

mind! Now I have V. G. Sevenby back again, I forgive you. You can come home once more.'

'No!' said Minnie. 'Virgil can do as he likes, but I prefer it here. I am dedicated to looking after sick pot plants. I have a career, Father, and I shall not give it up.'

How beautiful she looked, tossing her green curls! With her green ear she could hear the pot plants cheering her on, and that helped her to cope with the look of deep disappointment that crossed her father's face.

'But you will marry me, darling Minnie, won't you?' pleaded Virgil Sevenby. 'If you refuse, I shall never play the french horn again.'

'Well, I might,' said Minnie. 'I'll think about it. After all, we are only up to duet fifty-seven. We have nine hundred and forty-three to go. We might get through them more quickly if we were married. Besides, I think I love you, and that makes all the difference.'

Minnie and Virgil did get married. They started a new line of pot plants called the Sevenby Greens, and, three times a week, they played with Garfield Fortune's city orchestra, which was greatly improved by the addition of a harp and a french horn. As for the carnivorous pot plant, it became a reformed character, and lived on soya beans, protein extract and other herbal nourishment. Garfield Fortune's plants quickly recovered, and, though Minnie's hair finally went back to being golden, her ear stayed a bright green, and she was always able to hear the green voices of the world and secrets that nobody else knew.

It is safe to say that there was no town in all the world where there was better understanding between men and pot plants, and many people took to bringing their pot plants to the evening concerts, so that they could listen together to the golden tones of the french horn or the music of the harp sifting through the air like the soft, silver rain of a happy summer.

ELEPHANT MILK,
HIPPOPOTAMUS CHEESE

————— ☼ —————

There was once an orphan called Deedee who had the biggest feet in the world. They were so big she had grown extra strong ankles and knees in order to pick them up and put them down again. These enormous feet were a great embarrassment to her, and to the matron of the orphanage, as well. She didn't like having such a big-footed orphan clumping around her. She thought it spoiled the look of the orphanage.

Now, just down the road, there lived a man and a woman who were so lazy they had not washed the dishes for three years. Dirty dishes were piled up to the kitchen ceiling, down the hall, and along the garden path. It was lucky for them they had been given so many cups, saucers and plates when they were married. However, one morning they got up and looked around and found they had run out of clean dishes.

'What *shall* we do?' cried the man. 'We positively can't wash all these, and yet there isn't a clean dish in the house.'

'Ring up the orphanage,' suggested his wife, 'and we'll adopt a daughter to wash our dishes for us. Then, when she's done, we'll eat clean again.'

'What a good idea!' cried the man, and he rang up the orphanage at once.

'Have you got a girl orphan who can cook and clean all day, and half the night as well?' he asked. 'I don't want one that needs a lot of food or sleep, but I want one that's a good, strong, steady girl, because there's a lot to do around here and my wife and I are very delicate.'

'Yes, yes,' said the orphanage matron. 'We have just the orphan for you. Her name is Weedy Deedee. She won't eat much. She's little and thin, but she's got such big feet she's as steady as a rock. I'll send her round in a brace of shakes.' Then she went to the window and called, 'Deedee! Deedee! Weedy Deedee! Pack your bag and sign the book. You've been adopted by the people down the road.'

Weedy Deedee came clumping down the road from the orphanage, her big feet looking particularly enormous in their blue sneakers. She was about as tall as a rosebush, thin as string, with hair like bootlaces and feet like rowboats, but she had gentle, hopeful eyes and a lovely smile.

When she saw the dishes all the way down the garden path she sighed and set to work. She washed cups and

saucers, bread and butter plates, dinner plates, soup bowls, pudding bowls, mugs, glasses and tankards. She rinsed knives and forks and spoons, and then scoured saucepans, soup-pots and frying pans. She washed dishes all the way up the garden path, all the way down the hall and all the way through the kitchen from floor to ceiling. Finally, every dish was clean and every spoon sparkling.

'What next?' asked Weedy Deedee for she knew there was more to come.

'Dear adopted daughter Deedee,' said the man. 'You may do the washing.'

'And then the ironing!' said his wife.

'Make the beds!' commanded the man.

'Polish the furniture!' cried the woman.

'Chase the spiders!'

'Swat the flies!'

'Sweep!'

'Dust!'

'And then when you've done that, you may weed the garden,' the man concluded.

It looks like a full morning, thought Weedy Deedee. So she set to work. Though she was little and stringy she was strong at heart. She washed and ironed, made and polished, chased and swatted, and swept, dusted and weeded. The house shone like a treasure as much to be looked at as lived in.

'That's that!' said Weedy Deedee. 'And now, dear adopted parents, may I please have something to eat because I'm very hungry, and it's a long way past my dinner time.'

The man and the woman looked at each other in dismay. They hadn't reckoned on feeding her.

'She's very small,' said the man doubtfully.

'Except for her feet!' the woman muttered. 'I've heard that those with extra large feet eat extra large dinners in order to maintain them.'

'And she's worked very hard, too. She must be tremendously hungry by now,' the man said. 'Never mind! I have an idea. Leave this to me.' Then he turned to Deedee. 'Dear adopted daughter,' he said, 'we have a delicious meal of roast turkey and cranberry sauce, not to mention three colours of jelly and ice cream for pudding. But your dear adopted mother and I have one more job for you. We want you to paint the ceiling.'

'It certainly needs it,' said Deedee. 'Where's the ladder?'

'That's the problem. We don't have a ladder,' said the man with a horrid smile.

'Then I'll stand on the table,' Deedee said.

'What!' cried the woman. 'Stand on my beautiful, polished, mahogany table with your whopping great feet? Never!'

'But I can't reach the ceiling!' exclaimed Deedee. 'I'm too small.'

28

'Oh dear,' the man said, shaking his head. 'So you are. How tragic. You'd better go back to the orphanage until you've grown taller. How sad. It breaks our hearts. And you've done so well too, up until now.'

'That's it,' said the woman. 'Come back when you're taller.'

'You're still our dear adopted daughter and we'll think of you fondly, and pray for the day that you grow about three feet further towards the ceiling.'

Weedy Deedee hadn't unpacked yet. She clumped all the way back to the orphanage with her change of clothes and her toothbrush in a small case. But when she got there the gate was closed tight.

'Off you go!' said the matron, popping her head out of the window. 'We got another orphan in the moment you left, and there isn't any room now for you.'

'What shall I do?' asked Weedy Deedee.

'Anything you like!' said the matron. 'You're as free as a bird. Ah, freedom . . . freedom . . . would that I were as free and as happy-go-lucky as you!' and she popped her head back in again and locked the window . . . just to make sure.

So Weedy Deedee was turned loose on the world to wander and wonder. The roads of the world were very dusty and long, but luckily at that time of the year they were very pretty, all tangled along the sides with buttercups, daisies and foxgloves. She wandered and she wondered for quite a long time, until even *her* feet became sore and tired, in spite of being big. So when she came to a clear stream, its banks all tall with foxgloves, Weedy Deedee sat down on the bank, took off her blue sneakers, and put her feet into the water where they floated like two great white fish among the cresses.

'Oh, I'm so *hungry*,' sighed Weedy Deedee. 'I could eat a whole fried elephant, and still have room for a hippopotamus in chocolate sauce for pudding.'

Funnily enough, just as she said this, an elephant came round the corner of the road and then another and another until there was a whole herd of elephants eating up the buttercups and daisies. Then a hippopotamus came round the corner, and another and another, until a whole herd of hippos was waddling by, all smiling and beguiling in the afternoon sunshine.

Then came a different sound of feet, really big feet this time, feet that were certainly even bigger than Weedy Deedee's. She could hear them coming down the road and around the corner, and the thought of bigger feet than hers so terrified her that she jumped up and tried to hide in a clump of foxgloves. She was so weedy she fitted in among the foxgloves easily ... all except her feet, of course. They, poor lonely things that they were, had to stay sticking out into the world where everyone could see them.

Suddenly the herdsman – owner of the herds of elephants and hippos – came around the corner. He was definitely a giant, young and probably very handsome, except he was so big it was difficult to take him in all at once. By the time you got to his nose you had forgotten what his eyebrows were like. He had a lion bounding beside him, a kind of working dog. He saw Weedy Deedee's sneakers looking like blue canoes, moored among the buttercups and daisies on the bank of the stream.

'What beautiful shoes!' he cried wistfully. 'Oh, if I were to find the feet that fitted this footwear I know I would love them.' Weedy Deedee couldn't help wiggling her toes through sheer nervousness and the movement caught the giant's blue eyes.

'What beautiful feet sticking out of the foxgloves,' he exclaimed in amazement. 'What rounded rosy heels, what wonderful wiggling toes! If I could meet the maiden attached to these adorable extremities, I would make her

mine. These must be the most beautiful feet in the whole world.'

Weedy Deedee couldn't help laughing.

'They're the biggest, anyway!' she cried, looking out through the foxgloves.

The giant stared at her in astonishment. Then he began to laugh, too. The lion licked Weedy Deedee's feet and made them tickle, so that the laughing went on for some time.

'Well, that's life!' said the giant at last. 'I find a pair of feet to love and they're attached to little Deedee, who is no bigger than a rosebush. Never mind! Come out of the fox-gloves, for there's no need to hide. The lion's tame and so am I. The elephants and the hippos can wallow and graze, and you can sit down and share my lunch with me.'

'That would be wonderful,' said Weedy Deedee, 'because I've had a really full day so far. I was adopted first thing this morning, then I washed three years of dirty dishes, and tidied a very untidy house. Then it turned out I wasn't tall enough to paint the ceiling, and I had to go back to the orphanage until I grew three feet taller. But, meanwhile, the orphanage had got another orphan in my place so I was set free as a bird, and I wandered and wondered my way here. I'm as hungry as a hippopotamus, for I haven't had a bite or sup all day.'

'It doesn't bear thinking of,' said the giant, and passed a slice of cheese as big as a tea tray, and a cup of milk as large as a bucket, while his elephants grazed around eating the buttercups and daisies, and the hippos had a nice wet wallow under the willow trees.

A strange thing happened. As Weedy Deedee ate the cheese and drank the milk she thought that her feet had suddenly grown smaller.

'Look at that!' she cried. 'My feet have suddenly gone all little. What a pity! Up till now my feet were the only bit of me that anyone has ever admired.'

'They haven't got smaller,' said the giant. 'It's you who've grown taller. It must be from drinking elephant milk and eating hippopotamus cheese. After all, that's what I've eaten all my life, and look at me. You've actually grown about three feet taller.'

'What?' cried Weedy Deedee. 'Do you mean that I've grown tall enough to paint the ceiling . . . just when I was enjoying myself?'

'Oh, forget about that!' said the giant. 'Stay here and grow even taller and marry me. I've got a castle up on the hill with a garden full of sunflowers. Be mine and we will herd elephants and hippos together and garden, and have forty-nine children – seven times seven – and live happily ever after.'

Now she was a bit bigger, and could take in rather more of the giant's enormous face, Weedy Deedee could see he had a nose she liked and trusted.

'That sounds like a wonderful life,' she said. 'But I'd better paint the ceiling first, and tell my parents that I'm getting married. After all they did adopt me this morning, and my mother might like to help me make my wedding dress. I've read that that's what mothers do. I'll go home, paint the ceiling and get the wedding dress, and then I'll come back to you.'

'Take some milk and cheese to eat on the way,' said the giant. 'I've plenty left.'

So Deedee put some milk and cheese into a bundle, put on her blue sneakers, and set off over the roads of the world, golden in the evening sunlight.

The man and the woman who had adopted her were eating a dinner of roast turkey and cranberry sauce. Three colours of jelly, as well as ice cream, stood waiting for their attention. Dirty breakfast and lunch dishes were piled on the clean bench. Deedee looked at them sternly.

'It's our darling adopted daughter back again so soon,' said the man uneasily.

'And she's grown!' remarked the woman sourly. 'She *has* grown. She's grown enough to paint the ceiling, after all. It shows what you can do if you put your mind to it.'

'The paint pots are in the wash house,' the man said.

Deedee mixed the paint and cleaned the brushes. Without any trouble at all she painted the ceiling, while the man and the woman watched her, throwing the turkey bones over their shoulders.

'Dear adopted mother,' said Deedee while she painted. 'I

33

am going to be married, and I thought you might help me make my wedding dress.'

'Me!' screeched the woman. 'Me make a wedding dress for a weedy, not-so-little Deedee who I've only just met today. Think again!'

Deedee did think again, and looked very seriously at her darling adopted mother.

The man smiled at her weakly. 'Have a wing of turkey!' he said. 'Only a wing! There isn't a lot of meat on a turkey and my wife and I – we're very delicate, you know, and the doctor said . . .'

'Thank you! I've brought my own supper,' Deedee replied, and she poured her elephant milk into a tall vase and put her hippopotamus cheese on a platter before her.

'What's that?' asked her adopted parents greedily.

'Elephant milk and hippopotamus cheese,' Deedee told them, and she drank every drop and ate every crumb.

Suddenly her feet looked a lot smaller and the ceiling a lot closer. Weedy Deedee was weedy no more. She grew up through the house. Her arms went out through the windows, her head burst through the ceiling. Stretching towards the sky she felt the whole house lift off its floor and fold around her a wedding dress of wood and tin, shining with polish and paint.

Down below on the floor the man and the woman sat among their great set of dishes, dirty and clean, staring at her with terror. Weedy Deedee had grown, at last, to match her feet.

'Get your great feet out of here!' shouted the man, sounding as whining as a spiteful gnat. 'Get out, get out, you diabolical Deedee!'

'I'm going! I'm taking my feet where they will be well and truly appreciated,' Deedee replied calmly. 'And don't call me Deedee anymore. Call me . . . Désirée!'

Back up the road went Deedee-Désirée wearing the wedding-dress house, until the roads of the world led her to

the giant's castle. The giant came down through the sun-flowers to meet her, his faithful lion bounding at his side.

'I was waiting for you,' he said. 'What took you so long?'

'Painting the ceiling!' said Deedee-Désirée with a laugh. 'This is the only wedding dress in the world with a painted ceiling.'

So they were married, and together they washed dishes and weeded gardens, herded hippos and milked elephants. They had seven times seven (forty-nine) children who played among the sunflowers. And these children grew to be the most beautiful and happy giants in the land, with bright eyes and the nicest feet in the world – and so they should have been, for they lived on elephant milk, hippopotamus cheese, and a handful of sunflower seeds whenever they felt like a change.

CHIBBAWOKKI RAIN

—————— ☼ ——————

There was once a boy called Ethelred who was ready for anything. He lived in a town right next to one of those big jungles full of tigers, crocodiles, ruined cities and stone images tangled with vines. The town, on the other hand, was like all towns, full of supermarkets, banks, and light industry. It had a lot of market gardening on its outskirts, and towards the square in the centre – with its fine, stone statues – there were many gardens and notable lawns.

Now the town was the town and the jungle was the jungle, but they both needed rain to be comfortable, and it was many weeks since rain had fallen. As for the town, it was so dry the gardens crackled like brown paper. People walking through the square noticed the statues had their tongues hanging out because even they were thirsty. And as for the jungle, it was beginning to look crisp around the edges, as if it had been under a grill. (Ethelred, of course, took all this in his stride, because he was a boy who was ready for anything.)

Not everyone in the town, though, was ready for anything. The gardeners weren't ready for this great drought, and they complained about it day in, day out.

'It's because of the lost tribe,' they said to one another. 'Before that tribe went and lost itself there was none of this trouble. It rained every second night, a lovely soft rain that filled the tanks and kept the cucumbers coming on nicely.'

Ethelred's father was the noted Professor Maldive, a

neglectful and absent-minded father, but highly admired for his cleverness. However, *he* wasn't ready for anything. (Ethelred had inherited that from his late mother.) For months Professor Maldive had been searching for the lost tribe – he even had a university grant to help him to find it. However, up until now it was still lost. The strange thing was that Professor Maldive had a history of losing things in the jungle himself. He had once lost his twin brother, Bodley, curator of the museum, in a ruined city, and he hadn't ever managed to find him. All the same, with a university grant and a class of clever students, he had firmly expected to locate the lost tribe almost at once. But the tribe was well known for being dappled green and gold, and shadow grey, and, once you got into it, so was the jungle. It had turned out to be a lot harder to locate than he expected. Now the university grant had all been used up on mosquito netting, jungle boots, and medicine to cure snakebite and so on, and the tribe was still lost. They had simply vanished, taking all the rain with them. Even their name was not remembered. At least nobody seemed able to remember it now.

The weather got drier and drier. Nobody could have a bath. They all went to wash in the swimming pool which was out of town (because of all the shouting and splashing that went on in it), and right on the edge of the jungle. Every evening a long queue of citizens with their soap and towels and flannels waited to get into the sparkling water. Unfortunately, the water not only became more and more soapy, but it also sank lower and lower. Then, one day, a lot of crocodiles came trundling out of the jungle, pushed their way past the ticket office without paying, and took over the swimming pool. There was no arguing with them, for they were all bad-tempered, particularly as the soapy water stung their eyes. It was not what they were used to.

So no one was very happy. The gardeners weren't happy;

the university wasn't happy; the crocodiles weren't happy.
The only person in town with a light heart was Ethelred. He
was as dirty as anyone else, but it didn't worry him as much
because he was ready for anything and besides, he had a
wonderful hobby. Since his father was away at the university so much, Ethelred was amusing himself. He was
teaching himself to tap-dance from a book called *The Tap-
dancer's Instructor.*

After school, Ethelred hurried home, anxious to get on
with a very new and difficult step called *goats-in-the-kitchen.*
The street was filled with the sounds of gardeners moaning
and complaining, but, underneath them all, Ethelred's quick
ear heard a new voice talking to itself.

'Chibbawokki, Chibbawokki, Chibbawokki rain!' It was
rather catchy. Ethelred listened again.

'Chibbawokki, Chibbawokki, Chibbawokki rain!'

The speaker was a stranger in a suit of blue sacking, sewn
all over with various pockets. There were many unusual

things in these pockets as well as the usual sort of things – unpaid bills, various handkerchiefs, poppies, puppies, and coloured pencils. Not only this, the stranger was hung around with all sorts of objects on chains and strings: bugles, drums, medals, models, and a wide variety of lucky charms. He was staring in astonishment at the new town hall. Then he stared very narrowly at the museum. He looked as if he were just on the point of remembering something important and, as he struggled to remember, he muttered, 'Chibbawokki, Chibbawokki, Chibbawokki rain!'

Saying these mysterious words he stepped out in front of a bus. The bus driver speeded up. But Ethelred, who was ready for anything, seized the stranger by his large pockets and pulled him back on to the pavement, while the disappointed bus roared by, tooting its horn.

'You have saved my life!' the man shouted, clinging to Ethelred. 'How can I repay you? You must let me force you to accept a very, very, very large reward.'

'All right!' Ethelred agreed, because after all he *had* saved the man's life, and he thought he might as well have a very, very, very large reward since one was being offered to him.

But the man, drying his eyes, looked at Ethelred carefully and said, 'On the other hand I see you are not very big. Perhaps a small reward would be more in keeping.' He fumbled around, and then took from round his neck a small, black drum. He stared at it as if he were sorry to give it up, and then said aloud, 'Well – why not? I could never ever get it to work, anyway. It's yours – all yours. Don't try to thank me. And now, goodbye! Goodbye!' and he somehow managed to lose himself in a shop doorway crowded with people, all looking sadly at a photograph of a bath full of water.

It would be idle to pretend Ethelred was not slightly disappointed. Just for a moment he had almost been the possessor of a very, very, very large reward, and instead he had

wound up with a small, black drum that had never worked. However, Ethelred was ready for anything. A drum was better than nothing. He took it home with him.

There was no one at home, of course. Professor Maldive was away trying to talk the university authorities into giving him another grant. Ethelred was used to that. He put on his tap-shoes, and his powder-blue jacket with sequins on the lapels, and his straw boater, and he went out into the paved yard in front of his own back door. On either side of him, neighbouring gardeners stood weeping over their wizened crops, hoping that the tears would do some good. Ethelred laid *The Tap-dancer's Instructor* open on the paving, and put his feet in the correct starting position. He actually still had the drum hanging around his neck. Something echoed in his mind, and, instead of counting, he began to tap with his fingers on the drum, and his feet on the stone, and as he did this he said, 'Chibbawokki, Chibbawokki, Chibbawokki rain!'

A faint mist formed over his head, and he heard his feet talking to him more clearly than he had ever heard them before. 'Chibbawokki, Chibbawokki, Chibbawokki rain!' he said once more, just to encourage them. The mist became a small, black cloud, and when he said it a third time, there was a tiny (but fierce) flash of lightning, and a rumble of thunder so small it sounded as if a mouse were growling. Then it began to rain on Ethelred, though it was only like a sprinkling from a fairy watering-can.

'Come and dance here beside my cucumbers!' called the gardener next door, staring at him in amazement. 'Never did I think to see the day when I would be pleased to have a tap-dancer hoofing around among my cucumbers!'

Now tap-dancing in a dusty garden between shrunken cucumbers loses a lot of its charm, but Ethelred was an unselfish boy (and was ready for anything, besides). He danced, and tapped on his drum, and sang, 'Chibbawokki, Chibbawokki, Chibbawokki rain!'

The cloud grew bigger and growled more fiercely still. The rain fell a little more heavily.

'Here, come and do my tomatoes next,' said the neighbour one house along, gazing over the fence with a jealous expression. 'They're suffering something cruel. They're only the size of peanuts.' Ethelred was ready to take pity on the stunted tomatoes. This gardener had a nice bit of brick laid under his clothes line. The Shuffle-Off-to-Buffalo sideways step came out particularly well, even though Ethelred had to duck to avoid the underpants and socks hanging on the line. The cloud grew to the size of a bed quilt when it heard the beat of the Shuffle-Off-to-Buffalo sideways step, and the thunder was loud enough to blot out the sound of the drum.

Then gardeners from this street, and that street, and the

one beyond that, flocked around Ethelred, and he danced for petunias, marrows, gherkins, and poor, frizzled-up lawns. And then other people came asking him to dance in *their* streets. Up and down, in and out he went, down short streets, long streets, shabby streets, snobby streets. And everywhere he went, the cloud followed him like a black, growling bear. Everywhere Ethelred's feet talked to him, and his fingers pattered, and his drum spoke while he sang, 'Chibbawokki, Chibbawokki, Chibbawokki rain!' Ethelred just had to join in too. Other people quickly picked up the words, and some of the agile ones tried the Shuffle-Off-to-Buffalo sideways step with painful results.

Out at the university, Ethelred's father sat with his head in his hands moaning, because he had just heard that his university grant had been taken away from him. His students drifted away like leaves in autumn.

'How I wish I'd spent time teaching my little boy to play cricket,' moaned the repentant father. Just then the lightning played peeping-toms outside his window, and he heard a growl of thunder. He ran to peer out into the day and saw, storeys below, a large, low, black cloud. Dancing beneath it, so that the rain that fell from it irrigated the marigolds outside the university office, was a dashing coat in powder-blue with sequins on the lapels, and in the coat was his son, Ethelred. Professor Maldive opened his window and heard, faint but clear, Ethelred's voice far down below. 'Chibbawokki, Chibbawokki, Chibbawokki rain!'

'Why, I do believe that's the name of the lost tribe,' he shouted, striking his furrowed brow with his hand. 'How can it be that Ethelred – but no – but yes – even now it might not be too late!'

With exclamations such as these, he ran out of his office only to find the university lift was out of order. He had to run down eight floors, and by the time he reached ground level, the rain cloud and Ethelred had gone. Professor

Maldive stared around wildly, and saw the black cloud now raining somewhere in the direction of the park. The fountain there had only that morning been trickling out a little bit of brown soup, but now it leaped up, tall and sparkling, and wonderfully watery.

But, standing by the fountain, Ethelred was not quite as ready as he had been a little earlier. His feet were blistered, his taps worn thin. But school friends and acquaintances clustered around him shouting, 'Do the swimming pool next, Ethelred!' He couldn't bear to disappoint them.

Within five minutes he was dancing and singing around

43

the edge of the pool, 'Chibbawokki, Chibbawokki, Chibbawokki rain!'

The crocodiles snapped their jaws at him at first, but when they realized what good work he was doing they grew as docile as kittens. So Ethelred danced and drummed, and drummed and danced, and the swimming pool filled up little by little, while the children – all of whom had learned the chorus – sang with him, 'Chibbawokki, Chibbawokki, Chibbawokki rain!'

The air felt soft and smelled sweet once more. All over the city there were the sounds of plants drinking, and water soaking, and birds singing, for when it is too dry all nature suffers. The children took off their shirts and let the rain fall on their skin, and they shone like gold and silver – all except Ethelred who was terribly soggy in his powder-blue jacket. 'Chibbawokki, Chibbawokki, Chibbawokki rain!'

Just as he thought he could not dance another step, a hand fell on his shoulder. It was the man with all the pockets, most of them now filled with water and fish and frogs and waterlilies.

'How did you get that drum to work?' he asked. 'It's never worked for me. Give it back to me and I will give you a very, very, very big reward.'

Ethelred hesitated, for he had heard that story before. People shouted, 'Don't give it to him!' The children and crocodiles began closing in. But at that moment there was a great disturbance at the ticket office. A hundred enormous men and women, all seven-feet high and dappled green, gold and shadow grey, had burst out of the jungle, and into the swimming pool, and now they advanced in a long line, dancing and kicking and singing, 'Chibbawokki, Chibbawokki, Chibbawokki rain!'

Some paid for their tickets with bananas, pineapples, papaws and parrots, not to mention the occasional mango, but others merely threatened the ticket collector with little axes, and the cowardly man let them in at once. They surrounded the many-pocketed man and frowned at him very darkly.

'This is the man that stole our rain drum,' said their leader, a chieftainess of magnificent appearance. 'You told me you were only borrowing it for ten minutes, and you've been gone a year. You must now prepare to die.'

That is not the sort of thing that should ever take place in a public swimming pool.

Fortunately, at this moment, Professor Maldive and his students burst into the swimming pool area, using their season tickets to get past the ticket collector, still trying to do his duty.

'There you are!' cried Professor Maldive to his students. 'There is the lost tribe of Chibbawokki. I told you we would find them.'

The students burst into a round of delighted applause at this evidence of original research.

'We followed the sound of our rain drum,' said the chieftainess. 'We found the drum and also the black-hearted villain who stole it from us. We are going to have our revenge right here and now.'

'Mercy, mercy!' cried the many-pocketed man, writhing on the edge of the swimming pool. 'I will offer you a very, very, very large reward if you let me go. I only wanted it for my museum. I would have honoured it and sacrificed goats to it. It would have been very happy there.'

'Why, that is my brother, Bodley!' cried Professor Maldive. 'Found at last! Bodley, is that really you?'

'Wilmott?' cried the many-pocketed man, scrambling to his feet. 'My twin brother, whom I lost in the jungle? I've been looking for you ever since, Wilmott. I just turned my back and the next moment I had lost you.'

'No, no, Bodley. I was the one who lost you,' said Professor Maldive firmly.

'And there is the noble boy, ready for anything, who saved my life,' went on Bodley, introducing Ethelred to his own father, while the chieftainess patiently stood there, feeling the edge of her axe.

'That is my son, Ethelred,' said Professor Maldive proudly. 'When he took up tap-dancing, I confess I was disappointed. I wanted him to be a chemical engineer. But see what light feet and a light heart can bring about!'

'Your son? My nephew? Then this must be the city where my museum is,' cried Bodley, searching through his many pockets to find a handkerchief and failing to do so. 'The city doesn't look the way I remember it.'

'Enough!' said the chieftainess. 'He has stolen our rain drum. Now he must die.' She brandished her axe.

Things looked black, but though Ethelred's feet were covered in blisters he was once more ready for anything.

'Oh, great Chieftainess,' he began (a good beginning), 'leave it to us to punish him. He will be shut in cells of stone to which the light of day rarely penetrates, surrounded with the bones of long-dead animals, and broken pieces of pottery,

46

and made to label scraps of old metal and glass, and pieces of volcanic rock. He will do this all day.'

Bodley understood that this meant he would be given his old job at the museum back, and he nearly smiled with rapture. But, just in time, he remembered, and looked despairing instead. To the freedom-loving Chibbawokki tribe it sounded a terrible punishment.

'If that's the case we'll say no more about it,' said the chieftainess. 'However, we must have our rain drum back.'

Ethelred passed it over at once. They inspected it for damage, muttering among themselves. Then the chieftainess turned to Ethelred.

'We have our own dancing, of course, but we'd like you to give us tap-dancing lessons from time to time. Tap-dancing looks a lot of fun. We have no money, but perhaps you might be persuaded to accept a few diamonds as payment.'

Ethelred was so pleased that he did the Shuffle-Off-to-Buffalo sideways step very successfully, in spite of his blisters. The tribe and the assembled gardeners murmured in admiration.

'Who would have thought,' said Professor Maldive in rather a jealous voice, 'that tap-dancing would work better than a university grant?'

And ever after that, when it was too dry in that particular town, Ethelred would set off to find the Chibbawokki tribe and they would all do the Shuffle-Off-to-Buffalo sideways step chanting, 'Chibbawokki Chibbawokki, Chibbawokki rain!' and rain would fall all over the town's gardens.

It proved impossible to get the crocodiles out of the town swimming pool, though, and they had to build another one right beside it. It had a deep diving pool and an ice-cream parlour attached, and many was the happy afternoon that Ethelred spent there with his friends, the Chibbawokki tribe, watching the rain fall all over town. So everyone, including the crocodiles, lived happily ever after.

CAT AND MOUSE

One summer's day, a young mouse set out looking for adventure.

'Be very careful!' said his mother. 'It's a dangerous world for mice. Watch out for traps, and watch out for the sharp claws of the cat and, above all, don't be too sure of anything.'

As the mouse ran in and out of the stems of the sunflowers a cat saw him and called out in a sweet voice, 'Hello there, Mouse!'

The mouse stopped, hearing his name called, and looked out nervously.

'Come on out, Mouse, and talk to me,' the cat said. 'I'm rather lonely, and I'd love a bit of company.'

'But aren't you a cat?' asked the young and innocent mouse.

'A cat? Perish the thought!' cried the cat piously. 'I am none other than Santa Claus. Look at my white whiskers and white eyebrows if you don't believe me.'

The mouse had heard that Santa Claus had white whiskers and white eyebrows, and also that he gave people presents.

'Are you absolutely *sure* you're Santa Claus?' he asked, because there was still something about the cat that made him very suspicious.

'Of course I am,' said the cat. 'Look! Here are my claws to prove it. That's why I'm called Santa Claus. Come on out. I have presents and things for you down the path.'

As the mouse came out from among the sunflower stems, the cat pounced on him, catching him straight away.

'You should never believe everything you hear,' the cat said, 'because now I am going to eat you up.'

'You said we'd talk together,' cried the terrified mouse, realizing he had been tricked.

'Well, we'll talk a bit first if you like,' said the cat. 'And then I'll eat you up afterwards. I have plenty of time, and I'm not terribly hungry. I just like the thought of catching a mouse.'

The mouse thought very quickly.

'What makes you so sure I am a mouse?' he asked. 'You're not very clever for a cat.'

'Well, you *are* a mouse,' said the cat.

The mouse made himself laugh very hard. He didn't feel much like laughing. He just made himself laugh through sheer willpower.

'I'm not a mouse,' he said, when he had finished laughing, 'I'm a dog.'

It was the cat's turn to laugh, but it was a very surprised laugh. He had never caught a mouse like this one before.

'I know a mouse when I see one.'

'No – I'm definitely a dog!' declared the mouse, still

laughing, 'and when I get my breath back, I'm going to bark at you and chase you up a tree.'

Inside his mouse-mind he was telling himself: I'm not a mouse . . . I'm a dog. I'm *not* a mouse. I'm a *dog*. He made himself think dog thoughts.

'Just imagine you thinking that I am a mouse!' he cried.

'Well you look *quite* like a mouse,' the cat said, sounding rather less sure of himself. The mouse was looking a lot more like a dog than the cat had thought at first.

'Let me hear you bark!' the cat commanded.

'Wait a moment . . .' In his mouse-mind he was telling himself: Think *dog*! Bark *dog*! Be *dog*! 'Well, are you ready?'

'Yes!' said the cat.

'Then stand back a bit because I don't want to deafen you with my barking,' the mouse said, and the cat actually did stand back a bit, though he kept one paw firmly on the mouse's tail. The mouse barked as well as he could, but it came out very like a mouse's squeak.

'There!' said the cat triumphantly, 'and I'm going to eat you straight away because I can see you're a very tricky mouse.'

The mouse did not lose his head, even though he thought the cat might take it off with a single bite.

'You really do have mice on the brain. It'll serve you right when I chase you up a tree.'

'Think *dog*! Be *dog*!' he muttered under his whiskers. He made himself laugh in an easy-going fashion.

As he spoke a strange thing happened to the mouse. By now he believed he actually *was* a dog. The cat, which had looked so terrible a moment ago, began to look small and silly. Cowardly, too! He felt *dogness* swell up inside him. He thought he could remember burying bones, fighting other dogs, and, of course, chasing many, many cats. He felt a bark swelling in his throat. He barked again.

My goodness! the cat thought. He really *is* a dog, and here I am with my paw on his tail. The cat looked nervous and the mouse felt very strong. He opened his mouth and barked for a third time. This time there was no doubt about it: it was a really wonderful bark. The cat took his paw off the mouse's tail and ran for the trees with the mouse chasing him, barking furiously. The cat shot up the tree like a furry rocket and hid among the leaves.

Whew! That was a narrow escape, thought the cat, cowering at the top of the tree.

Whew! That was a narrow escape, thought the mouse at the bottom of the tree. 'I'm off home to Mother!'

As he reached the mousehole he saw his mother, nervously collecting sunflower seeds outside.

'Mother!' called the mouse. 'Here I am, home again.'

'Ahhhhh! A dog!' screamed his mother and popped down into the mousehole.

The mouse lay outside in the sun with his paws stretched in front of him and his tongue hanging out.

'Think *mouse*,' he panted. 'Think *mouse*!'

So he thought *mouse*, and, as he thought *mouse*, the *dogness* died away.

'What am I doing sitting out here in broad daylight with my tongue hanging out?' he squeaked to himself. 'I must be mad. That cat could come back at any moment.'

Then he scuttled into the mousehole where his mother met him with great delight.

'I'm glad you're back,' she said. 'It's dangerous out there. A big dog ran at me, barking.'

'A cat caught me,' the mouse said, 'but I escaped.'

'Escaped? Oh, my son! How did you manage that?'

'Cleverness,' said the mouse modestly. 'Cleverness and courage. I chased the cat up the tree.'

Exaggerating again, thought his mother, fondly.

Then the mouse and his mother had a delicious dinner of sunflower seeds.

As for the cat, he stayed up in the tree all day for fear of the savage dog that was waiting somewhere below in the summer garden.

THUNDERSTORMS AND RAINBOWS

———— ☼ ————

This is a story about a town called Trickle – a babbling, bubbling, swishing, swashing, murmuring, meandering kind of a town. And in this town lived a lovely young policewoman called Geraldine Busby, the one representative of the law in Trickle. Geraldine had been born in Trickle, and she loved it dearly. She wanted travellers and tourists to enjoy its strange beauties, too, but they practically always went over it or around it, because Trickle was a town with a problem.

Whenever relations visited people in the town of Trickle (which they did very reluctantly), they always put up their umbrellas and began by saying, 'Goodness, it *does* rain here, doesn't it?' Which it certainly did. For Trickle was the rainiest town in the world.

There were a lot of good things about it which people could have mentioned. It had a wonderful drainage system, for instance, but somehow there aren't many people interested in drains. It was also the greatest manufacturing centre for umbrellas in the whole country, from plain gentlemen's black to enormous umbrellas for families of ten, covered with lovely pictures of moons and stars, or printed with cheerful jokes which you could read from underneath. The National Gumboot Championships were always held in Trickle, but this, too, somehow failed to catch the public

interest. Even the municipal fountain was little known and appreciated, though it should have been famous. Most towns have fountains that shoot elegant sprays of water into the air, but in Trickle, where so much water was coming down already, the fountain shot fireworks, spinning catherine wheels, soaring rockets and big, gold-and-green sparks that flew up like birds and then burst into showers of lights. The children of Trickle, watching from their windows, loved to see these lights fall away like fiery moths and then go out, one by one. It was remarkable. It is only possible to have a firework fountain in a very damp town, you see. It is too dangerous in a dry one.

The sound of water was everywhere. It purred on the roofs and purred in the guttering. It sang in a thousand voices in the moats and canals, and in the conduits and culverts that ran round Trickle. It dashed along ditches, grumbling to itself, and chuckled in channels, plinked off edges, plunked off points and had so much to say for itself that no one could ever feel lonely in Trickle. Very few people in Trickle understood the water's mysterious, flowing language, but one of them was Geraldine Busby, the police-woman.

Of course you couldn't grow vegetables in Trickle – except for watercress – but people had gardens all the same, filled with rushes and reeds and pink waterlilies. And though there were very few cats to be seen in Trickle, there were many kind and affectionate frogs for the children to play with, as well as flotillas of white ducks with orange beaks, not to mention elegant herons and ibises. So there were plenty of pets to keep the people of Trickle company.

As for games, apart from swimming there was water-tennis and water-cricket, and water-football and water-hockey, and though the streets were seldom dry enough for bicycles, they were ideal for boats. Children went to school in canoes, mothers and fathers went to work in gondolas, yachts, punts and rafts – whatever they enjoyed most.

But you know what people are. They always think the place where they happen to live is the best place in the world, and the people in Trickle were no exception. They wanted visitors to enjoy their town's water pleasures, and to say how sorry they were to leave. But the polite ones always said, 'Goodness, it *does* rain here, doesn't it!' and the rude ones said, 'I can't wait to get out of this soggy, boggy, sopping, dripping, swampy, splashy puddle of a place,' and went off on the ferry without even waving goodbye.

This made the Tricklers very bitter, and their town council passed a law forbidding visitors to make any remarks about the rain. It was the job of policewoman Geraldine Busby to

55

wait on the wharf and, if any visitor getting off the ferry said, 'Goodness, it *does* rain here, doesn't it?' she was to arrest them and put them in prison ... the only floating prison in the world. It was built on a big raft, and during stormy weather prisoners sometimes felt seasick, though they were, in fact, about two or three miles from the sea. It was useless to try to tunnel out because it was guarded by specially trained eels, all anxious to taste any prisoner who tried to escape. However, so few people came to Trickle that the prison was almost always empty, in spite of this stern rule.

The Tricklers did their best to tell the world how enjoyable life was in Trickle. They had postcards printed showing the firework fountain and the pink waterlilies, but though these were displayed in the best hotels and motels, no one seemed interested. There was never a great crowd of laughing holiday-makers with swimming costumes and snorkels on the ferry that came once a week bringing ice cream, sausages and other necessities of civilized life.

'If I don't get more custom than this,' said the landlord of The Merry Mermaid tavern, pouring out tankards of bog beer and glasses of watercress wine for the local inhabitants, 'I will have to close down.'

Everyone looked very gloomy, because no town wishes its tavern to have to close its doors, and not a sound could be heard except for the friendly purr of the rain on the roof, and the song of a thousand little waterfalls.

Meanwhile, down on the wharf, Geraldine Busby, in her policewoman's raincoat, was waiting for the ferry to come in.

'I do believe there's a traveller on board,' she said to herself, and sure enough there was. Sitting among the ice cream and sausages was a young man with a pack on his back, eating an apple and looking at the wharf – and indeed the whole town of Trickle – with hopeful eyes,

though what he was hoping for Geraldine could not begin
to guess.

She watched him narrowly as he disembarked from the
ferry.

'My goodness, it *does* rain here, doesn't it?' he said to
Geraldine.

'I arrest you in the name of the law,' exclaimed Geraldine
sternly, pointing to a notice stating that comments on the
rain were punishable by a week in prison. He was the first
tourist they had had in months, and it seemed a pity to put
him in jail. But, after all, the law is the law.

Still, Geraldine was sorry for him because he had looked
so hopeful, and because he had fair curly hair of a sort she
particularly admired, and so for supper she took him a tray
bearing a bottle of watercress wine and smoked eel. She

even had some herself, though she sat on the other side of the bars, of course.

'But why should anyone object to rain?' asked the young man. 'When I said, "Goodness, it *does* rain here, doesn't it?" I meant it as praise. I love rain and I was delighted to see so much of it, because of my hobby.'

'What is your hobby?' asked Geraldine, taking an interest in her prisoner as a good policewoman should.

'I collect thunderstorms,' said the young man. 'I travel around the world searching them out and observing them, and storing them up in my memory. I never grow sick of thunderstorms. And as I came up to the wharf, I looked at your town and I thought, "This is the place! I'll see a magnificent thunderstorm here, I'm sure of it." But then you arrested me.'

'The law is the law,' replied Geraldine.

'Yes,' agreed the young man, 'and it's a pleasure to be arrested by a girl with curls as black as thunder and eyes like lightning.'

'Talking of thunderstorms,' Geraldine said, blushing and changing the subject, 'this *is* a wonderful place for thunderstorms. Thunderstorms and rainbows! There are lots of days when it's only drizzling, and the sun comes out and everything gets warm and misty. There are rainbows everywhere. Then, suddenly, everything darkens. Great black clouds roll in over the hills and stare down at us in between fingers of lightning.'

'You have a lot of lightning, do you?' asked the young prisoner eagerly.

'So much that you can read a book by it. In fact lots of people rush off to the library during a thunderstorm,' Geraldine said earnestly. 'We get sheet-lightning and fork-lightning and a continuous roll of thunder – all boom and *basso profundo*, if you know what I mean.'

'I know exactly what you mean,' said the young man,

'and I honour you for the beautiful way you describe it.' He lifted his glass of watercress wine in a gallant toast to the lovely young policewoman.

'Well, I'm a bit of a poet in my spare time,' Geraldine said bashfully.

'My name is Philip, you know,' the young man said. (Geraldine *did* know, for she had had to write his name down when she arrested him.)

'I think that you have been telling people the wrong things about Trickle,' Philip went on. 'I've seen your postcards mentioning the fireworks fountain and the waterlilies. Very nice too, in their way ... But they don't explain what it's really like here. Suppose you were to invite people to come especially *because* of the rain, and not in spite of it. After all there are people who travel great distances in order to find some sunshine, and since this is a world of opposites there must be people who would travel a long way for rain.'

'Do you really think so?' asked Geraldine, her eyes lighting up like lightning. 'You think that, instead of keeping quiet about just how much it rains here, we should tell people boldly that rain is our main characteristic – our speciality, as it were?'

'I'm sure of it,' said Philip warmly. 'But we must get it all organized. Bring me some paints and paper, and another bottle of that excellent watercress wine, and sit just there on the other side of the bars where I can see you. Somehow you seem to inspire me with your wonderful thunderstorm qualities.'

Geraldine was glad to hear this. A policewoman likes to be of value to the community, and to help prisoners adjust again to civilian life.

It was but a little while after Philip's arrest that a whole series of posters was sent out from the town of Trickle in the care of certain responsible citizens. These citizens travelled

59

far, seeking out hot, dusty, and desert places – places of
constant sand and sunshine. And they stuck up their posters
praising the town of Trickle.

When did you last see a rainbow? asked the posters boldly.
Come to Trickle – the world's rainbow centre! And, *Travel to
Trickle and take in a thunderstorm.* There were colourful
pictures of rainbows and thunderstorms just to remind
people what they looked like.

Far away, sitting on a baking-hot beach, was a rich man
and his wife. Suddenly the rich man stiffened with pro-
found interest.

'Look!' he said to his wife. 'It's years since I saw a thunderstorm.' He stared wistfully at the poster.

'It's years since I saw a rainbow,' his wife agreed. 'Shall we go in search of one?'

'Let's!' said the rich man, and they rushed off to buy a ticket to Trickle, followed by a lot of other people, almost as rich, who had not seen a thunderstorm or a rainbow for years and years, either.

Soon the first ferry-load of thunderstorm-and-rainbow tourists arrived at Trickle. Philip and Geraldine stood on the end of the wharf issuing them with brightly coloured gumboots, and umbrellas printed with rainbows and flashes of lightning. They were taken by gondola straight to The Merry Mermaid tavern, and while they waited for the thunderstorms to begin, they had a good view of the firework fountain, and nibbled local delicacies ... delicious smoked eel, smoked trout, smoked salmon, smoked oysters, delicate freshwater lobster and, of course, lots of chips. The rich man and his wife were both very impressed with the bog beer and the fine flavour of the watercress wine.

'We never expected anything like this in our wildest dreams,' they said to one another.

Up over the hills loomed clouds of astonishing blackness. Across their swarthy surfaces lightning wrote its eerie lines.

'I'm sure it is a sort of electric poem,' said the rich man, enchanted.

'Yes,' said his wife, 'and if we were quick enough we might read what was written there.' She took his arm.

'We'll never be quick enough!' said the man in a curiously contented voice. 'Some things are meant to be mysterious for ever.'

Like a great burst of applause for the lightning's mysterious never-to-be-read poetry, the thunder clapped its giant hands and sang among the hills. All the echoes joined in and so did the tourists, watching the thunderstorm from The Merry Mermaid tavern.

Then the clouds burst about them, the rain poured down

and water spoke in urgent chattering voices, beating on the roofs, babbling along the guttering, quarrelling with itself in the down-pipes, then rushing on, gurgling and singing, to join the mighty chorus of the magnificent Trickle drainage system. Lightning wrote again across the sky, thunder applauded, water gossiped and sang. Everyone was delighted – more than delighted – overwhelmed. The storm carried all before it. Then it passed. The rain grew quiet, and out between a break in the clouds the moon shone, painting every wet surface, every raindrop, with shining silver.

'Oh!' said everyone, and indeed there was nothing more to be said. They watched in silence, drinking their watercress wine, and then went up to bed. All had amazing dreams.

In the morning the sun was out, shining down through rain that was little more than a mist in the air.

'There it is,' said the rich man's wife. 'A rainbow!' A perfect rainbow stretched over the town of Trickle. 'And a wedding, too,' she added.

Out of the church a handsome couple walked – she with her black hair billowing like storm clouds, dressed in a dress of greeny-blue that flowed and foamed around her, and holding a bunch of pink waterlilies and slender bulrushes; he, tall and handsome in his striped swimming costume. They came out of the church between two lines of policemen and women wearing handsome, official raincoats, holding bright umbrellas over them, forming a triumphal arch. Then they poled off towards their wedding breakfast in a gondola of the most romantic kind. A rainbow formed at the end of the arch, and tiny rainbows danced in the air like butterflies.

'My dear, this is a wonderful town,' said the rich man's wife. 'We must tell all our friends about it.'

And later, when they had put on their own swimming costumes and paddled in little canoes in and out of the pink waterlilies, feeding the ducks and swans and admiring the frogs which watched them out of round, golden eyes, they said it all over again.

'We'll have to come back,' they said.

Although the town of Trickle never became a great holiday centre, people began to visit it particularly for its strange beauties. Boating people began to come, too, for they could hire not only dinghies and canoes in Trickle, but gondolas, coracles, jolly boats, shallops, sampans, skiffs, punts and various yachts. There was plenty for boating people to enjoy.

But Trickle's favourite tourists, the travellers that Trickle loved best, were the members of the Thunderstorm Fan Club and the Society of Rainbow Lovers. These two fine clubs had members from all over the world. Their members came to Trickle tired and weary, but went away refreshed, for there is nothing more refreshing than a rainbow. And even if you never quite manage to read the electric poems lightning writes over the storm clouds, they are a reminder of the mystery and amazement of the world we live in – wet or dry.

HOW HONESTY STREET WON THE BEAUTIFUL-STREET COMPETITION

———— ☼ ————

The great city of Hookywalker was so famous that it was visited by a constant stream of tourists, many of them rich. They would arrive in droves at the airport and be whisked through the city in red buses, with the bus drivers (all of whom were musical) singing the praises of Hookywalker in pleasant, tenor voices.

The only difficulty was that the main street into town was Ditchwater Drive which was rather on the dull side. The bus drivers did their best, but it was hard work trying to make Hookywalker sound interesting when almost all that the tourists could see were concrete blocks and telegraph poles.

'We shall have to do what we can to brighten things up,' said the city council. 'Let's have a competition for the most beautiful street. The buses from the airport will be instructed to drive along the street that wins the competition, and tourists will arrive in the city square anxious to spend a lot of money immediately.'

The competition was announced, and many streets were eager to take part, for the prize was a year's supply of free groceries, a gold cup, and a chance to meet a lot of notable tourists – visiting kings, prime ministers and so on. A lot of clipping, hoeing, digging, and mowing began, and the gardens around the airport began to blossom like bowers.

Two streets were particularly anxious to win the competition. One was Honesty Street, a street full of particularly worthwhile people. The Reverend Concord lived in Honesty Street, and in the house next to him (the one with the blue gate), were Miss Dignity and her sister Miss Edwina Dignity. Then there were Mr and Mrs Goodness, Captain Rectitude (the animal tracker and big-game hunter), and many other people of the same quality.

'It's a pity about Number Ten,' people said. 'Honesty Street would be perfect if it weren't for Number Ten.'

In Number Ten lived Miss Celia Slipstitch, who had been a freedom fighter in the Anguish Hills and had been blown up by many bombs. She had hundreds of medals for bomb

66

disposals, and had been named Freedom Fighter of the Year in 1925. But now she was old and confined to a wheelchair. Her nephew, Marcus, a most artistic boy, lived with her and pushed her everywhere she wanted to go. Gardening was out of the question for Miss Slipstitch, but she didn't sit around complaining. Instead, some years ago, she had taken a correspondence course in knitting and crochet, and now she could knit tents, curtains, parachutes, hammocks, carpets, and other soft-furnishings. However, in spite of all this activity she sometimes felt bored.

'Soft-furnishings are not enough!' she was heard to complain. 'I need more challenging work.'

Marcus did not garden either but it did not matter very much because he and his aunt had put their entire garden down to grass, and kept a goat called Spiro who nibbled it short. They did have a few foxgloves, which unfortunately count as noxious weeds, but, apart from that, all the other flowers in the garden were painted by Marcus on the walls of the house, or against tree trunks and fences. The rest of Honesty Street could not complain, because, though these were not real flowers, they were certainly tidy, and neither dropped petals or faded. So, in spite of Number Ten, Honesty Street thought they had a pretty good chance of winning the competition.

However, crossing Ditchwater Drive further down was another street called Mischief Avenue and, though the people living there were very keen to be given free groceries and a gold cup, they were not nearly so deserving. The first house in the street belonged to Dr Iago Shifty, and next to him was Sir Humphrey Malice, with a private zoo in his backyard, then Mrs Lila Grudge, and the two Conrad Crooks, father and son.

Being high-minded and hard-working by nature, the people in Honesty Street toiled night and morning.

On the other hand, the people in Mischief Avenue had a lot to tidy up before they could even begin to make their street beautiful because it had been lined with empty beer cans, bones, old boilers and so on. The people of Mischief Avenue hated gardening, and so they stole flowering shrubs and bedding plants from the park whenever they could, and boasted loudly about the size of their sunflowers and hollyhocks.

Of course the hollyhocks in Honesty Street were much bigger and better. Even Number Ten did what they could to help. Marcus put up a board fence to hide Spiro the goat (who was rather disreputable), and painted the fence with wonderful roses. These roses were painted so skilfully that bees came visiting and Marcus had to get up early every morning to dab the fence with honey so that they would not become disappointed. It does not help your chances in a beautiful-street competition to have a lot of disappointed bees bumbling up and down trying to get honey out of painted roses. But though Number Ten did its best, being as eager for free groceries as any other household, nobody took Celia Slipstitch and her nephew very seriously.

'No thank you,' was all their neighbours would say when Miss Celia Slipstitch offered to knit jerseys for the marrows and waistcoats for the pumpkins. 'All the vegetables are round the back and not on public view.'

As the time for the judging grew close, the people in Honesty Street were almost sure of winning. There were just two things that might count against them. One was that people from Mischief Avenue would creep in at night throwing eggs, stealing plants, and writing insulting things about the great city of Hookywalker on the footpath with spray-cans of paint, so that Honesty Street looked as if it had no patriotic feelings; and the other was that, even with its beautifully painted fence, Number Ten looked out of place in the middle of the blossoming street. There was nothing that they could do about Number Ten, of course, but they could do something about the attacks from Mischief Avenue. They put on tin hats in case of egg attacks, made bows and

arrows in case of robbery, and took it in turns to do guard duty, watching night after night through the wee small hours. Even then Dr Shifty and the two Conrad Crooks tried climbing over a back fence, but Spiro the goat saw them and acted with great courage. After that they did not try getting over a back fence again.

The day of judging drew even closer. Captain Rectitude supplied flamingos for the lily pond, and Mr Goodness's cousin, who ran an art gallery, promised them several fine classical statues of Roman gods and heroes. Not only this, they painted the telegraph poles to look like pink-and-white peppermint candy and then planted petunias around each one. The effect was beyond anything you ever saw. The street looked so pretty, you could imagine putting cream on it and eating it with a spoon.

Over in Mischief Avenue jealous Dr Shifty climbed up a tree and watched them through his field-glasses.

'They are unloading classical statues from the back of a van,' he cried. 'Never mind! I have a wicked plan. Soon it will swing into action. I am waiting for the night after tomorrow night when it is the turn of Miss Dignity and Miss

Edwina Dignity to keep watch. I have a nephew in a corner shop who has told me their guilty secret.'

Over the next two days Dr Shifty continued to watch the loving care being lavished on Honesty Street. Captain Rectitude, not content with flamingos, brought in a dovecote filled with snow-white doves specially trained not to perch on statues (for nothing spoils the dignity of a classical statue like a bird perching on its head). Mrs Goodness ran her electric polisher over the road, and Miss Edwina, a professional manicurist, trimmed the edges of the grass.

'Just you wait!' said Dr Shifty, and laughed nastily to himself.

Then it was the turn of the Misses Dignity to keep watch over Honesty Street. They did a little archery practice on their lawn, put on their tin hats, and went to the sentry box. Little did they know the wicked blow Dr Shifty was preparing to strike – a blow which would ruin for ever their chances of winning the most beautiful-street competition and getting a year's supply of free groceries. They were ladies of the highest character but Dr Shifty knew of a certain weakness they had and was planning to use it to overthrow all Honesty Street.

After midnight the hours crept by slowly. The Misses Dignity grew very tired. Their eyelids grew heavy. Up in the sky the moon looked like a silver penny, while every flowering shrub seemed like a strange, fierce animal crouched in the dark. After a while the Misses Dignity could not be sure if they were asleep or awake. It was unnatural for these two cultivated ladies to be wearing steel helmets, anyway.

At about three in the morning there came a sound as if of fairy bells.

'I think I'm dreaming,' cried Miss Dignity.

'Me too!' agreed Miss Edwina. But this did not surprise them for they often dreamed the same dream anyway.

Still, they could scarcely believe their eyes when an ice-

70

cream cart appeared around the corner bathed in a rosy light. They both rushed for it. They were too honourable to leave their posts because of threats of violence, but they both thought they might be dreaming, and they loved ice cream so much they would do almost anything to get some. This was the secret flaw in their characters that Dr Shifty had learned from his nephew in the corner grocery. While they were away trying to choose between passion-fruit crush and mango ripple, Sir Humphrey Malice sneaked into Honesty Street and released two powerful and destructive

pigs, Nero and Nerissa. These pigs were Mischief Avenue's secret weapon. Even when the Misses Dignity, swollen with mango ripple, came back to their sentry box telling each other what a wonderful dream they had enjoyed, they did not see the two pigs careering through the lovingly tended gardens of Honesty Street, attacking petunias and primulas alike. With their muscular snouts they uprooted azaleas, roses and honeysuckle, wallowed in the lily pond, terrifying the flamingos, and broke into compost heaps looking for nutritious scraps. At last they fell asleep.

When morning came the Misses Dignity took off their tin hats, hung them in the sentry box and turned around to go home. Then, in the cold grey light of morning, they saw the state of Honesty Street, and they both screamed and fell to the ground in a dead faint. Every flower had been bitten off short, and every lawn was covered with pig tracks. The lily pond was nothing but a muddy hole, the flamingos and the doves had flown away, and the gutters were full of half-eaten marrows and cabbages.

The cries of the collapsing Miss Dignitys brought all the residents of Honesty Street to their doorways and then out on to the footpath, Marcus from Number Ten pushing Miss Celia Slipstitch in her wheelchair. Early as it was, this gallant woman was at work knitting a beautiful wall hanging, commissioned for the Hookywalker mayoral chambers.

'Who has done this?' cried Mrs Goodness. 'Look! There are the marks of hoofs everywhere!'

'It's that goat!' exclaimed Mr Goodness.

'Spiro is innocent – I swear it,' Celia Slipstitch declared, but people did not believe her. The trouble was that Spiro looked guilty. No matter how pure their lives, goats always look guilty of something.

'It looks as if we will have to go without free groceries this year, and try very hard next year,' Miss Dignity sobbed into her lace-trimmed handkerchief.

'We will have to learn to eat goat stew,' said Captain Rectitude, looking grimly at Spiro.

'Wait a moment!' exclaimed Miss Slipstitch. 'I learned a lot about tracking when I was a freedom fighter. None of these tracks leads to Number Ten.'

'That's true,' said Captain Rectitude, 'and now that I look at the tracks I can see very clearly that they aren't quite like goat tracks either. They lead to the compost heap at the back of the Goodnesses' house.' A moment later Nero and Nerissa were discovered side by side among the potato peelings and apple cores. They opened their little eyes and grunted in an amused fashion.

Everyone apologized deeply to Spiro, who forgave them immediately as far as anyone could tell.

'All is not lost,' said Miss Slipstitch. 'I have been thinking. The free groceries go to the prettiest street, not to the best gardens. Tidy up as best you can and meanwhile Marcus and I will do our best to devise a few decorations.'

'Aunt Celia, this may be your greatest challenge,' said Marcus, looking at her proudly.

There was something about the hopeful spirits of Number Ten that lifted the hearts of all in Honesty Street. They set to work at once and, by the end of the day, the street looked possible, if not perfect. Tourists might not be enthusiastic about such a street but they would not feel insulted by it. Nero and Nerissa were locked in the compost bin where they lay peacefully recovering from their late night. They certainly showed no wish to return to Mischief Avenue.

At the end of the day all the residents of Honesty Street were tired to the bone from working so hard. But there had been no sign yet from Number Ten.

'I knew they would not have a plan,' said Mrs Goodness. 'These artists are good-hearted but hopelessly impractical.'

'Well, at least we are tidy,' said the Reverend Concord. 'I

shall sleep late tomorrow. There is no point in putting out a guard tonight, and no point in getting up early to meet the judges. I shall have a good night's sleep and then begin to make plans for next year.'

One and all agreed that this was a sensible idea. In the distance they could hear a faint cackling. It was Dr Shifty in Mischief Avenue, spying on them through his powerful field-glasses.

'We shall now win easily,' he called down to his wicked companions. 'Hurray for free groceries and a golden cup.'

In spite of the fact that the people of Honesty Street were all sleeping deeply, even snoring from pure weariness, there seemed to be a lot going on that night. Little lights glowed. There was whispering and the soft clicking of knitting needles. Nero and Nerissa looked out of the compost bin with great interest while the rest of Honesty Street slept deeply. Of course they all slept late. People woke up but they did not get up. They just lay in bed moaning quietly and saying, 'If only things were different!' as we all do from time to time.

At nine-thirty sharp a fanfare of civic trumpets an-nounced the arrival of the city council judges. There was silence for a few minutes. Then there was a sudden burst of heavenly music as the Municipal Choir, accompanied by the City String Orchestra, burst into song. The inhabitants of Honesty Street rushed out of their houses in their coloured dressing-gowns (all looking very attractive, however, par-ticularly the Reverend Concord who was seen to have his distinguished grey hair in rollers).

Honesty Street had never looked so pretty before. There were borders of pinks, pansies and forget-me-nots. Whole bushes had burst into bloom overnight. Sunflowers grew tall under the Dignitys' windows, and the Goodnesses' house was alive with daffodils and snowdrops. It was not just summer. It was spring, too, and autumn, for chrysanthemums grew around the Reverend Concord's door, and wintersweet around Number Ten. Seasons were happening all at once in Honesty Street.

A distant howl of rage was heard, like a far-away fire-engine. It was Dr Shifty who had got up early to impress the judges, and to do a bit of gloating. What he saw caused him to fall out of his tree, badly bruising Sir Humphrey Malice who stood underneath holding the ladder steady.

'Congratulations, Reverend Concord!' exclaimed the Lord Mayor of Hookywalker. 'This will do more to boost the city than the discovery of oil.'

'What an idea!' exclaimed the councillors. 'Knitted gardens!'

Everything was knitted. The sunflowers were knitted. The moonflowers were knitted. Moss-stitch hid the scars on the tree trunks and wonderful, neat stocking-stitch in green covered the pig tracks that had besmirched the lawns of Honesty Street. Crocheted cockle-shells edged the path. The pool was filled with blue waterlilies knitted in special waterproof wool and, because a few knitted flamingos (in sunset-pink wool, four-ply) had been placed on the edge of the pool, the other flamingos had come back – so had the fat, white, cooing doves. Swarms of bees collected the honey that Marcus had thoughtfully dabbed on the board fence especially for their attention.

Further down Honesty Street a bus-load of rich tourists had stopped and were already putting in expensive orders for knitted gardens. One tourist from a very hot, dry country had already ordered seventy-two metres of knitted lawn.

'Knitted gardens!' cried the Lord Mayor again. 'A year's supply of groceries and a gold cup is not enough. We'll have a torchlight procession and a barbecue to celebrate this breakthrough in the tourist industry.'

That night the inhabitants of Honesty Street were taken through town in open cars and showered with rose petals.

Marcus and Celia Slipstitch rode in front, Spiro was led by Captain Rectitude, who had now taken a liking to the goat, while Miss Dignity led Nero, and Miss Edwina, Nerissa, for neither pig wished to return to Sir Humphrey Malice's zoo. Though the pigs had been far from helpful, it is the funny way of the world that things would not have knitted together quite as well without them.

Meanwhile, in Mischief Avenue, all the wicked inhabitants, faced with the prospect of having to pay for their groceries for another year, had all gone to bed early and lay on their beds moaning and crying, 'Oh, if only things were different!' (as we all do from time to time).

But things *weren't* different, and it served them right.

DON'T CUT THE LAWN!

Mr Pomeroy went to his seaside cottage for the holidays. The sea was right, the sand was right, the sun was right, the salt was right. But outside his cottage the lawn had grown into a terrible, tussocky tangle. Mr Pomeroy decided that he would have to cut it.

He got out his lawnmower, Snapping Jack.

'Now for some fun!' said Snapping Jack. 'Things have been very quiet lately. I've been wanting to get at that cheeky grass for weeks and weeks.'

Mr Pomeroy began pushing the lawnmower, and the grass flew up and out. However, he had gone only a few steps when out of the tangly, tussocky jungle flew a lark which cried,

'Don't cut the lawn, don't cut the lawn!
You will cut my little nestlings which have just been born.'

Mr Pomeroy went to investigate and there, sure enough, were four baby larks in a nest on the ground.

'No need to worry, Madam!' cried Mr Pomeroy to the anxious mother. 'We will go around your nest and cut the lawn further away.'

So they went around the nest and started cutting the lawn further away.

'Now for it!' said Snapping Jack, snapping away cheerfully. But at that moment out jumped a mother hare and cried,

*'Don't cut the lawn, don't cut the lawn!
You will cut my little leveret which has just been born.'*

Mr Pomeroy went to investigate and there, sure enough, was a little brown leveret, safe in his own little tussocky form.

'We'll have to go further away to do our mowing,' Mr Pomeroy said to Snapping Jack. So they went further away and Mr Pomeroy said, 'Now we'll really begin cutting this lawn.'

'Right!' said Snapping Jack. 'We'll have no mercy on it.'

But they had only just begun to have no mercy on the lawn when a tabby cat leaped out of the tussocky tangle and mewed at them,

*'Don't cut the lawn, don't cut the lawn!
You will cut my little kittens which have just been born.'*

Mr Pomeroy went to investigate, and there, sure enough,

were two stripy kittens in a little, golden, tussocky, tangly hollow.

'This place is more like a zoo than a lawn,' grumbled Snapping Jack. 'We'll go further away this time, but you must promise to be hard-hearted or the lawn will get the better of us.'

'All right! If it happens again I'll be very hard-hearted,' promised Mr Pomeroy.

They began to cut where the lawn was longest, lankiest, tangliest and most terribly tough and tussocky.

'I'm not going to take any notice of any interruptions this time,' he said to himself firmly.

'We'll really get down to business,' said Snapping Jack, beginning to champ with satisfaction.

Then something moved in the long, lank, tussocky tangle. Something slowly sat up and stared at them with jewelled eyes. It was a big mother dragon, as green as

grass, as golden as a tussock. She looked at them and she hissed,

'Don't cut the lawn, don't cut the lawn!
You will cut my little dragon who has just been born.'

There, among the leathery scraps of the shell of the dragon's egg, was a tiny dragon, as golden and glittering as a be-jewelled evening bag. It blew out a tiny flame at them, just like a cigarette lighter.

'Isn't he clever for one so young!' exclaimed his loving mother. 'Of course I can blow out a very big flame. I could burn all this lawn in one blast if I wanted to. I could easily scorch off your eyebrows.'

'Fire restrictions are on,' croaked the alarmed Mr Pomeroy.

'Oh, I'm afraid that wouldn't stop me,' said the dragon. 'Not if I were upset about anything. And if you mowed my baby I'd be very upset. I'd probably breathe fire hot enough to melt a lawnmower!'

'What do *you* think?' Mr Pomeroy asked Snapping Jack.

'Let's leave it until next week,' said Snapping Jack hur-riedly. 'We don't want to upset a loving mother, do we? Particularly one that breathes fire!'

So the lawn was left alone and Mr Pomeroy sat on his veranda enjoying the sun, or swam in the sea enjoying the salt water, and day by day he watched the cottage lawn grow more tussocky and more tangly. Then, one day, out of the tussocks and tangles flew four baby larks which began learning how to soar and sing as larks do. And out of the tussocks and tangles came a little hare which frolicked and frisked as hares do. And out of the tussocks and tangles came two stripy kittens which pounced and bounced as kittens do. And *then* out of the tussocks and tangles came a little dragon with golden scales and eyes like stars, and it laid its shining head on Mr Pomeroy's knee and told him

81

some of the wonderful stories that only dragons know. Even Snapping Jack listened with interest.

'Fancy that!' he was heard to remark. 'I'm glad I talked Mr Pomeroy out of mowing the lawn. Who'd ever believe a tussocky, tangly lawn could be home to so many creatures. There's more to a lawn than mere grass, you know!'

And Mr Pomeroy, the larks, the leveret, the kittens and the little dragon all agreed with him.

THE WONDERFUL RED 'MEMORY' STRETCH-WOOL SOCKS

───── ✸ ─────

There was once a boy called Sam Snowgrass who had fine, big feet for a boy his size.

'They are just like your mother's feet,' people would say, for his mother had fine, big feet too. His father, on the other hand, had small, dainty feet for a father his size. Indeed, when he had been a boy himself, and a pupil of the Jellybean Day School for Clever Boys, Mr Snowgrass had had the part of Cinderella in the school play for three years running, and all on account of his small feet. No wonder he looked back to his school days with deep feelings.

'It was a fine school,' he would say with a sigh from the heart, for he loved the stage, and the school had been the scene of his greatest glory. Now he was grown up, he manufactured grommets. But times were hard and his business was not going well, though he smoked a lot of cigars and had business lunches and did all the right things to make himself successful.

'If only I were down on the first floor – the floor just above the Banana Court branch of the Big Bank,' he sighed. 'Not many people are willing to come up forty-two floors to buy grommets.'

When he was worried and depressed he often thought

how nice it would be to be back on the stage acting Cinderella.

'I could bring more to the part now,' he muttered to himself. 'I am a deeper person these days.' Of course his feet had grown since then, but they were still small. They were more or less the same size as Sam's feet which (let me remind you) were rather large.

One day there was a sock sale in a big shop in town. All the mothers, anxious for cheap socks, rushed to buy. Sam's mother was there too, though she would rather have been at work. She had a most interesting job in the Dinosaur Room of the Science Library, where she fitted the bones of dinosaurs back together again. It was a wrench for her to leave the bones and go to a sock sale, but she knew her duty. Sam and his father both needed socks badly. Just by luck she saw the very socks she needed and bought four pairs of bright red 'memory' stretch-wool socks – 'socks that "remember" the shape of your feet,' said the notice beside them.

'Two pairs for Sam and two for his father,' sighed Sam's mother.

Every morning for the rest of the year Sam put on his bright red 'memory' stretch-wool socks and went to school. Off he went down Pudding Street, turned right into Sausage Row, caught a bus that took him down Meatpie Lane and let him off at Jellybean Corner, right next to the Jellybean Day School for Clever Boys (the very school his father had attended in his glorious youth). There in the school hall, among the oil paintings of headmasters, and boys who had been fatally injured on the football field, was a photograph of Sam's father dressed as Cinderella, just to prove the school took an interest in art as well as sport and education.

While Sam was wearing his socks to school, Sam's father was putting on his own bright red socks and running to catch his own bus. It went down Pudding Street, turned left into Fruit Salad Drive, continued on past the traffic-lights, and through the tunnel under the River Mincemeat. Then the bus went around the roundabout into Jam Place and stopped right beside the parking lot of the Banana Court branch of the Big Bank. Sam's father would get off the bus, go into the bank building and catch the lift to the forty-second floor. Directly outside the lift was a door with his name on it. Behind that door was his desk which was ten feet long and had seven telephones on it (all different colours), and a polite secretary called Horace Wintergreen.

Meanwhile, at home, Sam's mother bent bravely over the washing-machine, washing the socks Sam and his father had worn the day before. She spin-dried them and hung them out before she went to her own work. When she came home, her very first thought, even before she made herself a cup of tea, was to bring the socks in from the line and put them in the airing cupboard, so that they would be fluffy and dry for the next morning.

Things went on like this for several months and then, one fatal day, Sam's mother, her thoughts full of a new dinosaur (the Nevermaurus), became so excited that she mixed up the two pairs of socks. She gave Sam his father's socks, and his father, Sam's.

Well, the next day a terrible thing happened. Sam's father, who was leaving for work early that morning, went out more or less as usual. But his feet in their bright red 'memory' stretch-wool socks carried him past his own bus stop. They almost ran down Pudding Street and turned into Sausage Row.

'Help! Help!' cried Sam's father. 'My feet are running away with me.' But people merely looked at his bright red socks and thought, 'There's Sam, having one of his games!'

Sam's father tried to stop the socks by hanging on to a telephone pole, but his feet were very determined and pulled so hard the telegraph pole began to bend over, and he had to let it go in case it snapped off short. Then his feet rushed up the steps of the wrong bus, waited so that he could buy a ticket (for they absolutely refused to take him off again), and then marched to a back seat of the bus which then carried him down Meatpie Lane.

When it stopped at Jellybean Corner his feet carried him smartly over the road and in at the Jellybean Day School for Clever Boys.

'Stop! Stop!' cried Mr Snowgrass. 'My feet are taking me to school when I should be in my office with my telephones, writing out invoices for grommets.'

However, once the teachers had seen his bright red socks they all said, 'What a fuss Sam is making this morning!' and took no notice of him.

Meanwhile, back at home, Sam set off expecting to go down Pudding Street just as usual, but his feet in their bright red socks carried him straight to his father's bus stop and wouldn't let him go past it.

I'd better do what my feet want me to do, Sam decided.

He climbed into the bus when it came, paid his fare, and the bus carried him left into Fruit Salad Drive, stopped at the traffic-lights until they turned green, went through the tunnel under the River Mincemeat, and then around the roundabout into Jam Place where it stopped beside the Banana Court branch of the Big Bank. Sam's feet carried him through the parking lot, into the bank building, and then into the lift.

What's going on, wondered Sam, but his trusty feet in their bright red socks, having carried him into the lift, carried him out again at the forty-second floor, and through the door with his father's name on it.

'Hello, Mr Snowgrass,' said Horace Wintergreen. 'You are looking short today.'

'I'm feeling rather tall,' said Sam, as his feet carried him over to his father's desk which was covered in grommet invoices. 'Lift me on to the merry-go-round chair, there's a good fellow.'

Horace Wintergreen did this, and now Sam could get at his father's seven, coloured telephones. A green phone rang. Sam picked it up and said, 'Snowgrass here,' which was perfectly true, though he did not say just which Snowgrass was speaking.

In the meantime, Mr Snowgrass was having a hard day at school. For years, now, Horace Wintergreen had done his spelling for him. He had forgotten how to spell a lot of words, and got most of them wrong. Without his calculator he could not do the simplest sums. The desk was too small for him and he kept on banging his knees. Worst of all there was not a single telephone on his school desk. On the other hand there were no invoices for grommets, either.

'Sam, you are being very careless today,' said his teacher.

Mr Snowgrass lit a cigar to show how successful he was but it only made the teacher terse.

'No smoking in school! Put out that cigar at once, Sam!'

Meanwhile, on the forty-second floor of the Banana Court branch of the Big Bank, Horace Wintergreen was offering Sam a cigar.

'No, thanks!' said Sam. 'I think I'll do a bit of ringing up and ordering.' He had often wanted to use his father's telephones, and now he had a wonderful chance to do so. He dialled a number he had invented.

'Acme Goldfish Company,' said a voice.

'Snowgrass here,' said Sam. 'Rush over two hundred of your best goldfish as well as a tank for them to live in, and a year's supply of goldfish food.' Sam put the phone down. 'That's the way I do business!' he said proudly to Horace Wintergreen.

88

Sam's father was dancing a folk dance with Muriel Wheeze (one of the pupils of the Jellybean Day School for Considerate Girls, specially invited for folk-dancing lessons).

'Please, Miss Fillmore,' shouted Muriel, 'Sam Snowgrass is making himself taller than me.'

'I *am* taller!' shouted Sam's father. 'I'm not Sam, I'm his father.'

'Sam, I recognize you by your socks,' said Miss Fillmore. 'Now don't tower over poor Muriel. Shorten yourself at once.'

Sam was having a lovely time ordering things. He ordered a brass band to play cheerful music outside the Big Bank, and he rented a magician to perform tricks for people travelling

89

in the lift. But he wanted to order still more. 'The Banana Court branch of the Big Bank still needs a bit of brightening up,' he declared. 'Horace, look up the number of the Circus Hire People will you?'

Outside, one and all were delighted at the good entertainment being provided in the parking lot. People were listening and even dancing to the band, and many were so moved by the music that they came into the ground floor where the branch of the Big Bank was situated and opened large accounts. The bank manager was very pleased.

'This will look good in the monthly report,' he chuckled.

When the circus arrived and people began putting up trapezes and tightropes he was more than pleased. He was actually delighted (very rare in bank managers).

'Oh, if only International Grommets were on the first floor instead of Fraudulent Industries Inc.!' he was heard to cry, for he did not like his bank being so close to Fraudulent Industries at the best of times. They were a very dicey firm, and had painted all the first-floor windows black.

Meanwhile, at the Jellybean Day School for Clever Boys, Sam's father's feet had carried him out into the playground where he met none other than his old speech and drama teacher, looking frail but still very artistic.

'Why, Sam,' said this worthy man, 'you're looking very tall today.'

'I'm feeling rather small, Sir!' said Mr Snowgrass humbly.

'Ah, how like your father you look!' declared the old teacher. 'What an actor he was! His Cinderella brought down the house.' Mr Snowgrass was about to explain yet again that he was Sam's father when a great temptation swept over him. Why not pretend actually to *be* Sam and have another go at Cinderella, he thought.

'Oh, Sir, why not put on that wonderful play again?' he

cried. 'I may not have feet as small as my father's used to be, but I act very well. I could make people think my feet were small by the sheer beauty of my acting!'

'What an idea!' exclaimed the old teacher. 'Do we dare . . . But why not? I will go and speak to the headmaster at once.'

Back at the Banana Court branch of the Big Bank, a millionaire was delighted to find his car in the middle of a circus. Beautiful women on white horses blew him kisses. An elephant put its trunk in at the open window of his car and gave him a rose.

'What is going on here?' asked the millionaire.

'It seems the Banana Court branch of the Big Bank is throwing a circus party,' shouted a woman who was dancing with a clown to the music of the band.

'What a confident bank that must be!' exclaimed the millionaire. 'I shall transfer all my money to the Banana Court branch at once.'

He stopped his car, which was promptly covered in spangles and confetti, and strode into the bank. When the bank manager saw a millionaire come into the bank he was *more* than delighted.

'But the circus is not mine,' he had to confess. 'It was hired by International Grommets Ltd.'

'They must be doing exceptionally well,' said the millionaire, very impressed. 'Where are they? On the floor above this, I suppose.'

'They are on floor forty-two,' said the bank manager.

'Why are they so high in the air?' asked the millionaire. 'Who wants to go all the way to floor forty-two to buy grommets? Who is on the floor above this?'

'Fraudulent Industries Inc.,' replied the bank manager.

'Ah! One of my own firms!' the millionaire observed. 'Let me see, Fraudulent Industries will work just as well on the

forty-second floor. We'll shift them up, and bring International Grommets down to the first floor. I like their way of doing business.'

He went up in the lift. It was full of people watching a magician pull rabbits out of a top hat. On the forty-second floor a huge aquarium full of goldfish was being installed. The millionaire walked past the fish, and in at the door labelled, *International Grommets Ltd. S. Snowgrass, Manager.*

'Snowgrass, is it?' he said to Sam, still behind his father's desk on the merry-go-round chair. 'Snowgrass, you may be very short but I like your way of doing business. If you will move down to the first floor I will place firm orders for fifty million grommets and that's my final offer.'

'Only fifty million!' cried Sam scornfully.

'Well, a hundred million, then. And all my companies, even Fraudulent Industries Inc. will buy all their grommets from you in the future.'

'Oh, all right,' said Sam, for he was getting tired of the telephones and the merry-go-round chair. Horace Wintergreen nearly fainted for joy, but Sam spoke to him sternly and he quickly revived.

'Horace, be a good fellow and tell the goldfish people to set up the aquarium on the first floor instead.'

Sam had had a wonderful day. He had used all the telephones, brightened up the Banana Court branch of the Big Bank and had received a firm order for a hundred million grommets. Not only this, Horace Wintergreen had done all his spelling for him.

But how did it happen, he wondered. It must be the bright red 'memory' stretch-wool socks. All this time they have been remembering the way to work. Now my father and I have the same size feet, so can it be that I am wearing his socks, and he is wearing mine? How can I make sure they don't get changed back again? I'd much rather come here than go to school.

Sam's father was thinking, What a fine school this is – every bit as good as I remember it. But how did I get here? It must be the red socks. After all, they are knitted of 'memory' stretch-wool, and remember all sorts of things. These must be Sam's socks I am wearing. Now, suppose I wash my own socks tonight, I will be sure of getting the right ones back tomorrow morning and I will be able to come to school again. Poor Sam! The boy has rather large feet I'm afraid, and he's probably had to do my invoices all day. But it's every man for himself in this life, and I might never get another chance to be Cinderella after this one.

Sam's mother was absolutely delighted not to have to wash socks for Sam and his father. They each washed their own socks for months afterwards (and by then it was too much of a habit for them to change back again).

Of course nothing lasts for ever, and the socks did wear out, even though they were knitted of 'memory' stretch-wool, but by then it did not matter. Mr Snowgrass had made such a wonderful job of being Cinderella that he was offered the part of Hamlet on television, a part in which the size of the feet doesn't matter very much. As for Sam, he and the millionaire liked each other's way of doing business so much that they became partners, and built up an industrial empire manufacturing not only mere grommets but reciprocating sprockets and gnurdling tubes, and other things without which life would be absolutely unthinkable. Fraudulent Industries Inc. painted all the windows on the forty-second floor black, and went very happily on its secretive way. Mrs Snowgrass, once she was relieved of sock duty, shot ahead to become none other than Katinka Snowgrass D.D.Ph. (Doctor of Dinosaur Philosophy), the world expert on dinosaurs and their bones.

So everyone lived happily ever after, as people sometimes do.

BALANCING ACTS

———— ☼ ————

Every morning when the Queen of the country woke up, her first thought was about somersaults. She was not very old, only about twelve, and the Prime Minister was afraid she was rather light-headed, even when she was wearing her crown.

She would wake up in the morning in her flowery pyjamas and her night-time crown; she would leap out of bed; she would turn three cartwheels to start the day off right. Then she would do seven backward somersaults, one after the other, just like that!

Not many queens are as quick off the mark as I am, she would think with great satisfaction. What a pity there isn't more call for somersaults in a royal life.

She put four chairs together, two tall gilt stools on top of them, and the royal-bedroom rubbish basket on top of that. Then she would nimbly climb to the top of this pyramid and balance on one foot. Though she was too high to get the full effect of her reflection in the mirror, she could at least see that her toes were beautifully pointed.

Pretty good, thought the Queen proudly. Then she would stand upside down on top of the upside-down rubbish basket, first on two hands, then on one hand, then on her head alone, with her arms gracefully extended at either side. She never had a chance to practise that bit as much as she would have liked because the maid would invariably open the door and announce, 'The Prime Minister, Ma'am.'

In would come the little fat Prime Minister, looking as if he were wound up and running on wheels.

'Look!' the Queen would cry. 'Look what I can do!'

She would extend one arm and the Prime Minister would kiss her hand, though it was not very easy when her hand was upside down.

'Very notable, Your Majesty!' the Prime Minister would say in a sarcastic voice. 'However, I have called to tell you we have used up this week's supply of money. The country is desperately in need of more cash-flow.'

'Invent some more!' the Queen always suggested. She could not see what was difficult about that. 'Run off another lot! The notes could have a picture of me on them, standing on my head. It would brighten them up.'

'Money is bright enough as it is!' exclaimed the horrified Prime Minister. 'You mustn't interfere with the dignity of

money. Get down off the rubbish basket, Your Majesty, turn the right way up, and put on your queenly clothes. Then we'll put our heads together and see if we can't come up with something.'

'Put our heads together?' exclaimed the Queen in excitement. 'Do you mean that you will stand on the mantelpiece and put your head on top of mine, then slowly straighten yourself up so that your feet almost touch the chandelier? Watch out for the spikes on my crown!'

'I was not elected to do flips, Your Majesty,' said the Prime Minister with dignity.

'That's what you think!' mumbled the disappointed Queen.

'I came here to balance the budget,' said the Prime Minister.

'It's about all he can balance,' the Queen said to the maid in a whisper. Aloud she added, 'Very well, Prime Minister, I will put on my queenly clothes, find a pencil and be with you in two shakes of a lamb's tail.'

The Queen's queenly clothes were very grand. She wore a red silk sleeveless vest, and red silk knickers. She wore a gold satin dress, pink sparkly shoes, and a cloak of deep-red velvet, trimmed with white fox-tails. As well as this, she wore quite a lot of valuable jewellery – a ruby ring, a necklace of rare pink pearls, and a crown covered with large diamonds, all over a hundred carats in weight.

'You can't do much dressed like this,' she grumbled.

'A Queen doesn't have to do anything except balance the budget,' said the maid, looking respectfully at the crown. The Queen had often noticed that, when she was wearing it, people looked at the crown and not at her. This made her cross. Over the maid's shoulder she could see the neat palace gardens, and then the palace wall, and the big gates. At the gates was a sentry keeping the wrong people out and the right people in. Outside, there were many twisty city streets leading to the big park. In the park was a huge blue tent where the Acrobat and Elephant Circus showed its marvels every night. The Queen herself had been taken to see them only last week, but she had not enjoyed it very much. For one thing she had had to go with the Prime Minister and a few ladies-in-waiting, and secondly she was jealous of the girl in the ruby-red leotard who stood so gracefully on top of the human pyramid, waving a flag.

Now, every morning, that very girl, whose name happened to be Florrie, would read the paper carefully, muttering and exclaiming with disgust as she did so.

'The country is still losing money!' Florrie would say. 'I'm fed up with it. What's the Queen doing to set us on a sound economic basis? That's what I want to know.'

'Florrie love, isn't it time you were practising your flips?' asked her mother, Mrs Florino. 'You were half a beat behind with your triple somersault last night. You nearly dropped your poor father.'

'The country is going to the dogs!' cried Florrie, 'and you ask me about triple somersaults. What I want to know is why don't they have a National Cake Stall? There's always

98

money to be made from the cake stall at a school fair. If I was in charge, things would be done differently, I can tell you. When I said, "Jump!" everyone would jump, and we would soon be financially sound.'

All the same, Florrie would go and do her balancing and somersaulting practice. Others depended on her. Apart from her father and mother, who worked with her as part-time acrobats (known as *The Flipping Florinos*), there was her brother, Ferdy, a strange little boy with hair the colour of moonlight who had never said a word in his eight years. He was useless as an acrobat because he always seemed to be staring into the air as if he were watching butterflies no one else could see. The Florinos couldn't travel with the circus, but when it was in town they were one of its most famous attractions. The trouble with Ferdy was that, though he was practically always a little bit up in the air, he never really came down to the ground, and all acrobats have to do that sooner or later. So he did the housework and the cooking, but not wonderfully well, for he was always watching the skies for butterflies, or maybe angels. It was anyone's guess what he saw.

One morning the Queen woke unexpectedly early. It was as if an unexpected voice had whispered, 'It's now or never!' in her ear. It was one of those pearly early mornings when everything seems silky and new. The blue canopy of the Acrobat and Elephant Circus shone across the city, even over the palace wall, like the vision of a better life. The Queen thought of the Prime Minister and sighed. She thought of the bills, and of the budget that wouldn't balance, and of the maid, and of the cluttering, queenly clothes.

'Right!' said the Queen. 'This is it.'

She couldn't go out in her pyjamas, so she put on her queenly clothes herself.

At that early hour of the day the maid was dreaming of

99

grandeur, the Prime Minister was dreaming of taxes, and the sentry at the gate, who had just nodded off for a moment, was dreaming of bacon for breakfast. No one saw the Queen run out of the palace grounds and into the city streets.

She pulled off her ruby ring and threw it up into the air. Up, up it went, shining like a red star until it fell again, tinkling into the gutter behind her.

'Away with all that!' cried the Queen.

A moment later she tossed her pink pearl necklace into somebody's hedge. It hung there like a cobweb filled with drops of fabulous rain.

'Away with all that, too!' shouted the excited Queen, and,

robes and all, she did a cartwheel on the corner of the deserted street.

On that very same morning Florrie felt someone shaking her and waking her. It was Ferdy, pointing outside and looking, just for the moment, as if he might come down to earth, or even speak to her.

'Is the newspaper here yet?' asked Florrie. Ferdy shook his head. 'Then what is there to get up for?' she cried. 'Just more flip-flops and human pyramids, while the country goes to rack and ruin around me.'

But she got up all the same, put on her ruby-red practice-leotard and set out into the pearly early morning with Ferdy. Once she got out into it, she knew at once it was the sort of morning when anything could happen, although she was almost sure that nothing would.

'I've been doing somersaults for years,' she exclaimed, 'and all the time I could have been wearing rings like this one.' She picked up a lovely ruby ring from the gutter and put it on her finger as they walked towards a little back entrance to the big park. 'Suppose, for instance, I was able to wear pearls like this,' continued Florrie, pulling a necklace of pink pearls out of a nearby hedge, 'people would take me seriously. People would listen to my theories. But as it is – nothing!'

Ferdy nodded and danced around her, apparently playing with his invisible, butterfly friends. They entered the park together.

The grass was covered with tiny cobwebs for, overnight, a thousand little spiders had been spinning their own silk, dew had fallen, and now the lawns looked as if they had been covered with a thin film of quicksilver.

'If I were wearing shoes like these,' cried Florrie, putting on a pair of pink sparkling slippers that just happened to be lying on the edge of the grass, 'I could put my foot down properly and people would take notice.'

Across the quicksilver lawn raced a row of footprints. Bare feet had walked freely there, leaving prints that led into the trees and towards the circus tent, rising beyond the leaves like a new, blue sky. The true sky was still as clear and colourless as water. Florrie and Ferdy followed the footprints.

'A person like I am needs more to life than somersaults,' Florrie continued. 'Standing on the human pyramid and waving a flag is all right, but I need more people to lift me higher. Not that you'd understand, Ferdy, for you're a changeling and live according to different rules. It's like this: there are some that belong in a circus, and others that have a grip on financial life and ought to be given a chance. But you don't get a chance – not unless, perhaps, you're wearing one of these.' She picked up a gold satin gown that happened to be draped over the petunias, and absent-mindedly slid it over her head. It fitted exactly. 'If you're wearing one of these, people respect your judgement.'

Ferdy flung his arms and danced in admiration. Having no words to express it, he had to talk with his feet and fingers.

'I'd fix things up. Everyone would say, "Thank you, Queen Florrie." They'd say, "Now there's a queen who knows what's what!" And I'd sweep by in my crimson cloak with the white fox-tails around the edge – just like this one, actually, lying here.'

Florrie was wrapped in her dream of glory, and now she picked up and wrapped around her shoulders a wonderful, dark-red velvet cloak that just happened to be lying at her feet on the dry, curled leaves. 'Pretty good, eh?'

By now she looked almost entirely royal. They walked out of the shrubbery, and there before them was the circus tent, and rising up before its heavenly blue was a glittering sun.

'I'd say, "Do it!" and they'd do it, and we'd all be saved.

We'd become a prosperous nation, that's what. But it's not
likely to happen until I'm wearing a – gosh, that's lucky!
There's one right in front of me,' and Florrie picked a dia-
mond-studded crown like a rare apple ready for picking, out
of a tree. She put it on her own head, to a fanfare of morning
blackbirds. As she did so the sun rose and Florrie stood
there, glittering just like a queen or an expensive kind of
Christmas decoration.

Suddenly, out of the trees to her right burst the maid and
the sentry and the Prime Minister.

'Oh, Your Majesty, we were so worried,' they said. Ferdy
watched them as if they were the flitting butterflies of his
dreams and he saw clearly that they did not look once at

Florrie's face but only at the diamond crown above it. They did not see a real girl, only a dazzling queen.

'Here I am! I'll come right away!' the Queen said. 'Prime Minister, I want you to give me half an hour before breakfast, and, by the time I've finished, the budget won't merely be balanced, it'll be jumping through fiery hoops. It'll be playing "God Save the Queen" on tuned motor horns. And then I'll have a light breakfast of strawberries, candied oranges and cream.'

She gave Ferdy a stern look as she went off with them – stern, but pleading, too. Don't tell, will you, that stern but pleading look said.

Ferdy watched her go. He began to do one of his funny little dances and laughed as if he were sharing a joke with the air. Out of the shadow of the circus tent came a girl in a red silk vest and knickers. She smiled at Ferdy as if she already knew him well, and did twice-seven somersaults one after another across the grass, which no longer shone silver but glittered like a carpet set with thousands of pretty little jewels. Out of the trees on the left came Mr and Mrs Florino.

'Florrie and Ferdy!' they cried. 'How worried we've been! But oh, Florrie – what skill! We knew you were talented but we never dreamed you were as good as this. The circus might take us on permanently when they see how good your work really is.'

Ferdy noticed they were entirely busy looking at amazing flip-flops. They did not notice the real girl, only a wonderful, whirling cartwheel.

'Florrie,' they cried, 'fetch Ferdy and follow us home.'

But Ferdy was so delighted with all he had seen that pearly early morning (for he had seen two people fit into the very spaces that they had longed to find), that something untied his tongue and he spoke for the first time – strangely enough in rhyme.

'The children born right
Have refused to be left,
And there's nobody left to be wrong.
And I have the right to write down what I know,
Or to sing it aloud, like a song.

One turned to the left,
And the other turned right,
And they happened to cross in between.
So one will turn cartwheels and fly like a kite
And one balance books like a queen.'

Mr and Mrs Florino were delighted all over again, for it is a great thing to have a poet in the family.

And, many weeks later, when the country had some money once more and things were looking up, the Queen looked up too. She had taken all the children in the city to the circus that particular morning, and her eyes met the eyes of the girl in a red silk leotard on the very tip-top of the human pyramid. They smiled at each other like strangers who also happen, mysteriously, to be very close friends. Ferdy, the new poet of the city, thought he saw a little black butterfly of sadness fluttering in each eye, but life is short and no one can fit everything into it. We all have to learn to balance in our own particular way, and when people find the place that fits them best, and poets find words and rhymes and jokes to tell about it, there's a good chance that everyone will live happily ever after.